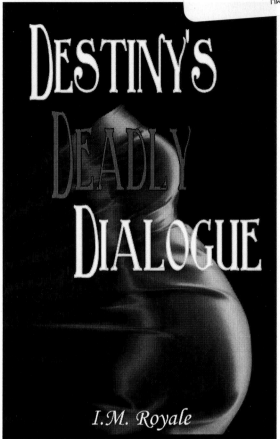

Copyright © 2007 by Imani Royale

Unless otherwise noted, all scripture quotations are from The NIV Study Bible, 10th Anniversary Edition New International Version Zondervan Publishing House, Grand Rapids, Michigan 49530 USA copyright ©1985, 1995, 2002

Library of Congress Control Number: 2007930374
ISBN 978-0-9773805-3-4

Printed in the United States of America 2007

Dedications

Bea Ayepong - My mentor

For we wrestle not against flesh and blood, but against principalities, against powers, against the rulers of the darkness of this world, against spiritual wickedness in high places.

~ Ephesians 6:12 (KJV)

*One day the angels came to present themselves before the
Lord, and Satan also came with them.*

~ Job 1:6

one

Gasping for breath Peter knew that death was upon him. As his eye lashes erratically flickered, he tried with all of his might to preserve his life. Sweat rolled down his face from his hair. His breathing became shallow and his heartbeat slowed down, he fearfully monitored every breath that was leaving his body. The hospital room was cold and grim. Along with the perspiration on his forehead, chills ran up and down Peter's arms, and he was shaking and confused at the contrast of sweat and cold that overtook him during the last moments of his life. Fear of the unknown caused his stomach to turn and his bowels to loosen. His mind was racing, thinking about his past. At this point, regret of not accomplishing something meaningful burned within his heart. He had heard about life after death many times, heaven, hell, reincarnation and purgatory, but after turning sixty he decided to ignore all of it. It was silly to him. But he couldn't help wonder what was in store for his soul in the afterlife, since he didn't believe in God at all.

Only when his wife was around had he pretended to accept what she believed. Wanting to keep peace in his home, he didn't challenge her belief. He simply went along with the program she had set in place for the family.

His thoughts were disrupted by the sound of shoes slapping the linoleum. The footsteps got closer and rounded the corner to his room. ---Oh no, here comes the old windbag again.

The head nurse entered and said, "You poor thing. I have a dose of pain killer that will help ease your discomfort. It will not be long before you enter into eternal rest. You are worn out. Try your best to calm down and take deep breaths."

Peter sighed loudly, signaling the nurse to shut up, in his way trying to let her know that he could hear her words of doom and gloom and didn't appreciate them one bit. ---Maybe if I clear my throat, the old beetle will clip her upper lip.

Peter was known in his better days as a bitter man who irritated the clerks at the grocery store. It was obvious to the nurse on duty that he was dying and still had not changed his ways based upon his sons description of him.

---How could I have allowed my life to pass away without ever telling my boy I loved him? Was I really a good father? I hate myself for not doing something meaningful like helping the poor, writing a book, or sharing some of my inventions. A legacy was always important to my father, and he worked hard for many years trying to build something great for his family, something that would last. I was lazy. I procrastinated and didn't bring out the ideas in my head. My God, there were many imaginings and every time they came to mind I intended on carrying them out, but the days and years passed with *nothing*, just excuses, excuses, excuses. I allowed great opportunities to slip through my fingers. I always thought I would live forever.

Peter's nose began twitching. It felt as if a tiny bug had crawled inside but he was too weak to go in after it and too sick to explain it to the nurse. He was also irritated by the dreadful smell of his hospital room. "This room smells like death he grumbled."

Tears ran down his face as he lay there hopeless and limp, without one last chance at turning his life around. Like the wind, his life was blowing away and he knew in his heart this was the end, a dead end.

Agony, more mental than physical, drained his skin almost bloodless. He was pale and his right hand was weak from the intravenous therapy the nurse had placed in it when he first arrived. John and Doris sat stoned-like continuing their vigil. John noticed that his father's right arm was streaked with dried blood and giving way to a dusty gray color. He was his father's only son. He moved closer. Peter reached over and touched his son's forehead. John looked over at his wife Doris and said, "He must be trying to tell me something."

Peter groaned, frustrated because he knew John couldn't read his mind or understand him through the saliva that seeped out when he tried to open his mouth. "Son please, don't be like me," he struggled. "Live life to the fullest and search for purpose. Do something that will help the generations to come. Don't ignore the tugging of your heart to do more. Never stand still. Brush all excuses aside that might hinder you from following your heart's desire. Make a difference and don't let your life pass by without causing change." But Peter's attempt to speak was unintelligible. John knew that his dad was trying to communicate something important to him. He could *feel* it in his soul. It was hard for John to understand his father's muffled words, so he remained patient and pretended like he understood as not to irritate his father. John remained attentive to the old man's desperate pleas.

Miraculously, Peter gathered up enough strength to spill out words that John could understand, "Believe in yourself son, and do what is good."

"Your dad is getting weaker, he is so pale," John's wife whispered.

A chaplain walked into the room and put her arm around John and asked if she could pray with him. John was dazed and really didn't feel like praying but he felt it was the right thing to do; besides he never had the guts to disappoint a man or woman of the cloth. The chaplain reached out for John and Doris' hands and prayed a prayer of comfort.

—

A glow came over Peter's face as he drifted into the unknown. Somehow that prayer made his transition easier. In his last minute he asked God to forgive him his wrong-doing. Peter envisioned a tunnel. Then a light appeared. A warm feeling washed over him as rays of light beckoned him to come closer. He felt loved and believed the prayer of salvation had worked on his behalf. He felt guilty for getting that speedy prayer through just before his heart stop beating, but he saw angels now and felt good that they were full of light and not the dark creatures he had seen in movies. Peter felt himself moving swiftly as if preparing for a race. The angels began to usher him into his new place.

"Peter, there is a great gulf fixed between heaven and hell, and you are never to cross over it. If you do so, disgrace and agony will be yours," said one of the angels. "Know that the place you will dwell is paradise. The Prince of Darkness is upset that you made it in. His eyes have witnessed the decision of your heart. Thank God you were truly sorry for your sins and your ignorance of God's will for your life. The words spoken from your mouth were spoken in truth and came from your heart. You almost missed the gift of eternity."

Satan saw another soul enter paradise that missed God's divine order for his life. He knew that when souls disobey God's plan, fear consumes them during the judgment. Satan watched this particular soul named Peter desperately hoping for acceptance after receiving judgment for his idleness while on earth. Satan was angry at the grace bestowed upon the new soul and the gift of salvation for his life. He flared his nostrils and sniffed Peter's scent. It reeked of fear. He was overjoyed that during Peter's earthly life, he didn't believe in God but was terrified of the devil. He knew God wouldn't be happy with Peter's failed faith. He glided over to Peter. Peter was unaware of Satan's presence. In a symbolic gesture of evil, Satan wrapped his form around

Peter and hissed into his ear, "Si vis pacem para bellum, Petri."[1]

Peter was experiencing the amazing colors in paradise, unaware of Satan's presence surrounding his spirit, when he suddenly felt nauseous and retched. Suddenly he was bent over with grief. He composed himself and shouted, "Sola Fide." Peter was confused by his own outburst and then heard a audible interpretation. "By faith alone."

"Be still Peter, and pay close attention. The Almighty is about to speak to Michael about a new life on earth that will concern you," said the angel Gabriel.

A deafening sound rumbled through paradise as God prepared to speak to his angel of protection, Arch Angel Micheal.

"Michael, you have served me well. Take this spirit of Ramla and allow her to be born. What are your questions?"

"Almighty God, what shall be Ramla's sex?"

"Female."

"Into which family line shall Ramla be delivered?"

"The Mayhem."

"In what part of the world shall Ramla live?"

"North America."

"What is her calling, most gracious Father?"

---

[1] Si vis pacem para bellum, Petri – Latin translated "If you want peace, prepare for war, Peter"

"Ramla has been designated as the "Repairer of the Breach." She will be a giver, a philanthropist, an agent for the poor, and one who uplifts humanity.

"And if she fails, what happens to the poor?"

"If she refuses to obey the calling that I have placed upon her life, many lives will be lost due to her disobedience."

"Father, her spirit is being placed with Mayhem, a lineage cursed for generations and beleaguered with poverty and addiction. How will she overcome?"

"My word will be spoken over Ramla's life and my spirit will strengthen her to bring my plans to fruition. Make sure that Isaiah 58:12 is prophesied over her life. This truth must be spoken in the earth realm. It is thus:

"Ramla will be used to remove the yoke of sin and repression that runs deep in many family lines. Her spirit will help awaken and strengthen others through her benevolence and charity. Her good works will bring the blessings of God as long as she is obedient to him and allows the Holy Spirit to guide her."

"Father it is done."

"When and if she activates the gift that I have placed inside of her, she will be known as a woman that can fix almost anything. She will have the finances to rebuild cities and renovate buildings so that the poor will have homes to live in and their children will have schools to attend."

"How will the world come to know Ramla?"

"Her gift will make room for her all over the world."

"God, where will the gift dwell?"

"The gift dwells in the center of one's heart in great abundance."

"Almighty, you are awesome. Your word declares that out of the abundance of the heart the mouth speaks. Ramla will speak her own destiny into existence."

"Yes Michael. My desire for mankind will flow through her heart and I shall bring great things to pass."

—

"Oh my, I can see the earth from here. Look! There is a man praying. Who is he?" Peter asked.

"That is a pastor of a great work. He prays many hours a day. Because of his diligence in prayer, the growth of his congregation is phenomenal, and miracles are a normal event for his parishioners."

"He is remarkable. The words coming out of his mouth are causing things to happen in the spirit realm. His words are coming alive. Who is that standing next to him?

"Peter, that's the Holy Spirit. He is doing his job in the spirit realm in order for the pastor's prayers to come to pass in the earth realm. Do you remember reading in the book of Genesis how God spoke the creation of earth into existence?"

"I have never seen anything like this before. Even the angels are moved by his words. You mean to tell me that every word I spoke while on earth caused something to happen in the spirit realm? If so, I'm doomed because I spoke so many negative things about myself and others. No wonder I struggled so hard to get ahead."

"Peter, the Bible was in your home. Great instructions for your life were plainly written. How was it that you missed the instructions that were there to guide you every step of the way? Luke 6:45 explained it this way, *The good man brings good things out of the good stored up in his heart, and the evil man brings evil things out of the evil stored up in his heart. For out of the overflow of his heart his mouth speaks.*"

"I am upset with myself. I completely ignored the obvious. If I had only known the power that was in the scriptures, I wouldn't have taken them for granted."

"Most don't take the Bible seriously. To them it is just another good history book. There are many beneficial books written by great authors, books that have plenty of scriptures to feed the soul, however what angels have witnessed shocks them. Many readers skip over the scriptures in the book in order to quickly get to the author's advice. Peter, I watched as you suffered many things on earth. Your finances and physical body were full of darkness. Your wife kept sending up prayers for you, the answers were sent to you daily but you did not have an ear to hear what the spirit of the Lord was saying. God gave a fine example of turning darkness into light. It is made clear in Genesis 1:1-4, *In the beginning God created the heavens and the earth. Now the earth was formless and empty, darkness was over the surface of the deep, and the Spirit of God was hovering over the waters. And God said, "Let there be light," and there was light. God saw that the light was good, and He separated the light from the darkness.* Peter, the evidence of the power of God's spoken word was right there in your living room gathering dust. Did you not believe its worth? How is it that its importance was missed? We angels are bewildered by the lack of faith men display regarding the Bible. If they knew how to operate in the wisdom inspired by God, their lives would change forever. In God's will and in his power, man has the capacity to produce prosperity for a specific purpose. What they say has influence. Proverbs 18:21 reads, *The tongue has the power of life and death, and those who love it will eat its fruit."*

"I'm sorry for not taking the Bible seriously."

"Peter you must stop focusing on your lack of understanding while on earth. It will slow down your progress. There are many truths that you are about witness as your learning takes place." You Peter will be referred to as the angel of faith.

"Wow does this mean I will be like you?

"No Peter you could never be like me, for I was created before the foundations of the earth. The word Angel in your case means guardian, and faith is the instrument you will use to overcome doubt and unbelief in order to gain victory.

Michael the arch angel paused and encouraged Peter to listen. "SOVEREIGNTY was about to speak."

—

God spoke to Michael so Peter could hear and understand, "Now go and prepare the musicians and singers that I have gifted to appear in the same generation as Ramla. She will need their gifts for emotional healing in order to pass through the fire of Satan's attacks. Not everyone makes it. Many will fall by the wayside, some are lazy, and others would rather choose their own way and experience eternal damnation. Music will be used to comfort Ramla's soul and strategically help her fight the tormentors that have been assigned to her life, especially when the people that I have called by name are in tune to the gift and realize the powerful source of it. I have purposefully anointed them to bring hope. Some lyrics will be used in the form of the spoken word to break down strongholds and deliver many from suicide. It is one of Satan's key weapons to stop my plan. The great deceiver is the one that leads the weary to kill themselves. Now go Michael and prepare the singers. I will give them the ability to communicate my love to the people that live on earth."

"It is done in your name. Amen"

Without hesitation, Michael spoke to all in heaven, "Ramla shall be born a female. Her family line is cursed for generations. God created Ramla not only to discover her destiny, but to bring relief to her bloodline and to support the poor of this world. Know that Satan will fight against her soul. He hates the will of God being established in an individual's life."

—

Michael took Peter, the newest soul in heaven, to witness the creation of Ramla. They ushered Ramla's soul to the Holy Spirit who would delivered her to a woman's womb during the time of conception. Michael gave instructions to the angel and he complied. It was time for Peter to observe what it meant to find one's destiny and be obedient. Michael advised Peter to be silent. Gabriel had a message for him.

"You are expected to meditate and ponder Ramla's life on earth. You must take time to reflect upon her trials and tribulations and discover how finding her destiny relates to you. You shall hear my voice again."

With that, Michael the Arch Angel was gone. Peter felt alone and a bit anxious. He wasn't clear on where he was.

He just knew that he was somewhere in paradise to observe the one they call Ramla. Peter's attention turned to a gentle ripple in a pond. It was the Pond of Contemplation. Somehow he knew that others had rested there before to learn. As he studied the ripples, he noticed a glimmer of light beginning to form. Jesus appeared before him quietly, yet with power. His body was surrounded by an intense white light. Peter experienced an overwhelming feeling of love. He immediately got on his knees before God.

"My precious child, you begin learning today. You were a good man in your earthbound life, yet you didn't pursue your destiny. You have been chosen along with several others in heaven to observe Ramla. She will be tested in her faith. You are to help guide her, but also observe and learn from her life as well. Because you were chosen for this responsibility, you will be held accountable to a higher standard. Go, be apart of Ramla's delivery process. There is much for you to see and even more to contemplate."

The Pond of Contemplation mirrored a woman as her womb was impregnated with the seed and spirit of Ramla. A fluttering of a hundred thousand angel wings was heard throughout heaven. Satan also perceived the flutters and knew Ramla would soon be born. The hairs on Satan's back stood up and frustration consumed him. This was the day he dreaded for many years. He made it his main goal to destroy the life of the one they called Ramla, by any means necessary.

Peering deep into the pond, Peter witnessed the child they call Ramla nestled within the womb. He suddenly was a part of her aura, part of her experience. Peter was one with her along with the other designated guardian angels. They were to be with her, every step of the way, including the birthing experience.

"Peter, as you watch Ramla's birth, you will feel as if you are actually undergoing the physical birth along with her. It is important to take in every detail," whispered the angel of destiny.

"I understand."

He knew he couldn't possibly grasp how difficult this would be. The hundred thousand angel wings fluttered again and Ramla's mother began to moan as she labored. Sweat was beading on her forehead and she was holding on to her husband's hand, squeezing it to help ease the agony of childbirth. Ramla's mother looked fiercely at her husband with eyes that blamed him for her pain.

Peter focused on Ramla in the womb. He felt his own body restricted in movement as she struggled to stretch and break herself free. He could hear muffled voices and sense darkness all around. He became warm and had the reassurance of tepid fluids all about him. Peter began to feel pressure as Ramla moved down the canal. It was more compact than where she had been. She was resisting and Peter felt claustrophobic. She continued to move downward, headfirst. The voices were still muffled, but getting louder. The tunnel put pressure on her and forced her along. Stifled noises suddenly became extraordinary roars. She couldn't see, but felt something cold and hard about her head and shoulders. The crown of her head full of beautiful red hair stretched her mother's vagina and made its way into a brand new world. A bright light pointed directly into her eyes. She couldn't breathe. At the pond, Peter gasped too. They both began to panic. Her mouth was pried open and her airway cleaned. A slap upon her bottom was met with a cry of freedom from her depths. Ramla had arrived.

A nurse carried the infant away. She cleaned, measured, weighed and noted the time of birth. She wrapped her in a cozy blanket and brought her to the mother.

"Congratulations momma. Is this your first?"

"Oh yes. She's beautiful. Look at all of that auburn hair—my beautiful baby girl."

"Is there anyone in your family that has red hair? The nurse asked.

"Well yes. My grandmother's hair was red but I never expected to have a baby with red hair. It's so soft, and such an intense red I might add. I think this girl might be someone special."

"Mother you look very tired. You will have a long time to cuddle and care for your little one. Let's use your days in the hospital to rest and prepare for your baby's early morning feedings."

The nurse took Ramla to the nursery so she could sleep and be monitored and so her mother could recuperate. Ramla's mother was groggy and starting to feel pain from the natural birth.

"Don't fret. We'll take care of that pain for you. Your little one needs her rest as well," replied the nurse.

As she prepared to roll the new mother to her room, the nurse noticed the beads of sweat on the mother's forehead and felt unusually warm herself.

"Faye, will you check the thermostat? It's awfully warm."

"That's funny, it says sixty-six degrees. It's supposed to be much cooler in here. I'll turn it down"

—

Satan had watched Ramla's birth with great interest. Upon hearing her freedom cry, he released his heated rage in a deafening roar to the child's guardian angels. "I am here, angels! Even the humans felt me. Little did they know I could have killed the ugly thing right then. There in the presence of all of you. I will wait though, and you will fail."

"Satan, we will not fail," replied the angel of destiny.

"You can't see me," smirked Satan.

"That is true," another angel acknowledged.

"Where is Peter, the one that I call boy?"

Peter startled and struggled to say his name but was muted by fear. He looked to the angel of destiny with a dread worse than any he experienced in his lifetime.

"Peter is here. You have no power over him. You are here to test Ramla, not Peter," replied the angel.

"Your Peter is afraid. His soul has been shaken and it quivers in silence at the very sound of my voice. I see you boy," Satan laughed. "Don't doubt me angels. I am more powerful than you. Remember, your foolish refusal to go with me from heaven even after I took one-third of your number with me. You were cowards then and you are cowards now."

Then there was silence. The guardian angels were enveloped in nothingness. Shaken, Peter looked up from the Pond of Contemplation and prayed.

"Dear Lord, please allow me to overcome my fear of Satan. I am terrified of him."

He lost himself in supplication and pleaded for deliverance, when he felt an illumination overhead.

"Dear child, do you doubt my love for you?" Jesus asked.

"No, Jesus. I'm just so afraid of Satan." Peter cried.

"Stand-up and fight your fear, my son. I have given you everything you need to succeed. Know that if fear remains in your heart you have not yet accepted my perfect love for you. You still hold onto guilt from your past. Release it and know that my grace is sufficient for you."

Peter wanted to be free of guilt and weakness but still believed he was a disgrace to his Lord. So he remained at the pool and pondered for a long time after Jesus left, begging for a mercy he wasn't sure he could accept, and for power to overcome the darkness. Images from long ago appeared and suddenly he remembered the pain of not feeling loved as a young boy by his father. If he couldn't have the love of his own father, how ever could he really grasp the love of Jesus?

—

Satan appeared again in the delivery room down the hallway, where another young woman was giving birth to Ramla's nemesis. He covered her like a sheet and found delight in her agony. She bore down, again and again, and cried out for help, for mercy, and for the deliverance of the child.

The doctor shouted to his medical team, "C-Section everyone. The infant is in distress."

A team moved in unison to quickly anesthetize the patient and assemble the instruments for delivery. As the doctor scrubbed and the nurses scurried to readiness, the woman screamed loud and more urgently than before. All eyes turned to her and the surgeon who would incise her huge belly saw that its flesh had been torn away, exposing the infant inside.

"Jesus Christ! Who made this incision?" yelled the surgeon.

The nurses froze in shocked silence but only for a moment. There was work to be done. The doctor reached inside to get the baby. He turned and lifted the boy from his mother careful not to go farther than the umbilical cord would reach. He looked, but no cord attached the child to its mother. Disbelieving, he looked again at the child that squirmed in his hands and then to his mother for signs of the trailing thing and finding none, handed the child to a nurse without comment or so much as a look of explanation. He had none. His medical training took hold and he moved to stitch the woman's belly back together. When he approached her, he saw that it had already been done. He bent close and inspected the neat and expert row. He looked at the others that would assist him. Their eyes said everything and nothing. The surgeon stumbled out of the room and fainted in the hallway.

Two nurses attended the child, suctioning and cleaning him. The air turned warm and started to stir. It accelerated to a wind that whipped their scrubs and sent gloves and gauze, and clips and clamps blowing around the room. Had the HVAC system run amok? Were the windows open? The nurses were petrified. One placed the child in a bassinette while the other ran to close the window, but the window was sealed shut. Outside, there was no sign of blowing wind, only trees tranquil and full of autumn color, and the small parking lot busy as usual with hospital staff and visitors.

Satan appeared before the glazed-eyed infant and lightly clawed three 6's into the boy's forehead. The child screamed but Satan silenced him and spit vile upon his heart.

"I am the prince of darkness. I am Satan, and you shall follow me as long as I deem. You will be named Sammael, meaning angel of death. You are poison. Your purpose is to inflict pain upon the one they call Ramla. You will do this for me in the name of evil."

—

Peter lifted up off his knees. In these hours, God had revealed his supremacy and now Peter was amazed and he somehow felt empowered. He knew why he was afraid of Satan. Even though Satan tried at times to tempt him during his earth years, he was known to Peter as evil. Everything he ever heard about Satan was wicked. He felt differently now, as he peered into the Pond of Contemplation. He was learning.

"Jesus, I now understand why I am afraid of Satan. "

As a child he would harass me, I was tormented me in my sleep.

Peter watched for a sign from Jesus but he didn't see one. He listened closely and continued.

"Why have you stopped communicating with me, Lord?"

Something led Peter back to his knees. Chills covered him and he stayed silent, waiting.

"Peter, I will make myself known to you in many ways. I haven't stopped communicating with you. You will learn to converse with me. Now rise with faith and believe for Ramla's total deliverance."

"Lord, I will do this in your name."

Peter began to relate with Jesus through his heart and soul. And, he learned that he found a part of himself that he never knew existed, a part that reached out to Jesus in spirit and in truth. Nothing was hidden, no secrets motives, no games, just pure unadulterated love.

Peter called to the angel of destiny concerning Ramla.

"Yes, Peter. Do you have a question?"

"No. I must guide Ramla through the trials of her life. It's imperative."

"Why, Peter? What has brought you to this conclusion?"

"Before destiny can be achieved, faith must be established."

"What about Satan? You are afraid of him. Before you can help Ramla with faith, you must establish faith within yourself. You must embrace faith."

"I understand. I am requesting that I be her guardian, a supernatural being on earth, to walk each step of the way with her. I am requesting to touch the hearts of selected people to assist Ramla. I am ready. Sola Fide."

Peter presented his case and believed he was a right choice. There was silence between him and the angel of destiny but he felt determined and wise, happy because he finally realized he was destined to use his faith.

"Go Peter and be with Ramla. It is so written and held in history with the keeper of the records."

Peter closed his eyes and whispered a prayer for strength and guidance, "Kyrie Eleisson, Christe Eleisson, Kyrie Eleisson."[2]

—

Ramla's mother was at a loss for naming her child. Heaven had already named her but as her earthly mother, she was not aware of this. She finally settled on the name Ramla not understanding why, it seemed as if the name was whispered in her ear. For some unknown reason, the sound

---

[2] Kyrie Eleisson, Christe Eleisson, Kyrie Eleisson – Latin for Lord Have Mercy, Christ Have Mercy, Lord Have Mercy

of Ramla swirled around in her heart and gave Eva a warm fuzzy feeling.

There was peace and a knowing set deep inside Ramla. As a child she was aware that her life would become more meaningful than most, but how could she know that every corner of it would be littered with temptation and sorrow.

—

Satan waited with great anticipation for Ramla's faith to be crushed. He sat in the shadows, just beyond sight and sound. The first of her trials would start in a little while. His appetite was whetted by machinations of her failure. The more horrid and complex his evil schemes for her became, the more he stank. Foul and rotten, putrid like no other. The angels were silent, listening for him. They knew the time was near. And then, a rabid growl came up from the center of the earth.

—

Satan inhabited Ramla's home. At night, he hovered above her bed taunting and mocking the child that God had created. Satan wanted to prove God wrong and so in the beginning, at the moment of freedom cry, he agreed to God's rule not to kill Ramla or her parents.

He passed like a zephyr through the wall of her parents' bedroom. They were sound asleep, curled together in their king-sized bed under too many layers of blankets, and totally unaware of what was going on in the spirit realm.

Satan swung low over them, approaching their heads with his hideousness. Into their conscience he planted, "You will hate each other. Davis will be with another woman and turn to alcohol. It shall rule your world and you will divorce." He licked them sweetly with his flames and rejoiced at their impending misery. Infidelity alone would rip them apart and shatter the foundation of their union and the security of their precious child and children that would follow.

two

amla's father labored to get out of bed each morning. He glanced over at his wife as her chest moved up and down in deep sleep. He felt like crying because he couldn't shake the feeling of doom and despair from his psyche. This year had been tough financially and he was turning up the bottle more than ever. It seemed as if hell was breaking loose in his home and that he no longer had control over the events that were playing out around him. Everything was in disarray.

"Mmmmm….Davis? What time is it?" Ramla's mother asked.

"Five o'clock in the morning. Go back to sleep, Eva."

She made no protest and rolled back over to sleep. Davis looked at his children's pictures on the dresser and sighed. They were too young for all of this, but he knew he couldn't go on forever. Eva had no idea that he wasn't working quite as much as he let on. Their marriage had disintegrated years ago and now they stayed together for the sake of Ramla and her brother Clay.

It seemed to him that Eva was getting deeper and deeper into the Jehovah Witness religion and he was growing tired of it. The long skirts and early morning walks through the neighborhood passing out the Watchtower made him uneasy. He was embarrassed for the neighbors to see his wife coming their way. She dragged their children along, training them in the ways of what he consider to be a cult. Nothing felt good to him anymore, except sex. Not so much with Eva, mind you, but with his mistress still fresh with the idea of being in love.

Davis slowly got out of bed and quietly shut the door. He took a shower and got ready for work. It would be just a matter of hours before he was sitting at Lucky's bar on the edge of town. It was better than watching Eva get the children up and herd them out dressed in old-fashioned clothes door-to-door preaching rubbish, or as she put it, the Bible according to thus and such. He had no interest in her newfound gospel—none at all.

Davis downed the first smooth shot of Jack and shoved the empty toward the bartender.

"Say man, don't you think you ought to slow down on that? It's only 10:30."

The bartender sighed as Davis impatiently tapped the glass.

"It's your liver, man."

He poured the shot and set about restocking the bar. Davis watched him disappear into the back room then leaned over the bar to replenish his drink. Lucky owed him a free drink now and then anyway, he was a good customer. He sipped it and thought about the probability of getting fired and didn't care. The bartender came around the corner as he poured himself one more and thought about Eva and the kids and how he felt trapped at a dead end. The second-shift boys were arriving and when Davis looked up at the clock he saw it was nearly five. He reached in his pocket for the fat wad of ones, threw them down, and staggered out of the bar. He drove toward home drunk and fast, barely missing a pedestrian who had stepped off the sidewalk. His life, his love, his luck, all were dead ends. It registered at some dull level but he'd think about that tomorrow. He stumbled into the house like Jack Daniels himself, tottering across the living room, singing "Groovy People". Tonight he was Lou Rawls. Tomorrow would come soon enough.

Eva was furious. She smelled him before she even saw him and knew he had missed work again. The sight of him repulsed her. She thought back to when they first met and how he wooed her, sang to her, and loved her sweetly. He drank little. He was a bear of a man, but tender with her and she felt protected in his embrace. She no longer felt sheltered, just pried open and exposed to the world. He passed out in their bed. Each day was the same, and Eva was getting sick of it. Most days she still tried to be the dutiful wife, but inside she brooded and beat against the lie.

"Davis, get out," she yelled. "I am fed up with you boozing all day and tired of all the rest of your crazy addictions you refuse to get help for. Just get out. Now!"

In no condition to argue, he headed to the kitchen and gathered some trash bags into which he deposited some of his belongings. Half-way to his car Davis begged Eva to let him stay, at least until he could find a place to live.

Eva walked over to the looking glass and stared at her features. She was an attractive woman with beautiful cream-colored skin, yet the reflection staring back at her was someone she no longer recognized. Saddened by the dark bags that sagged under her eyes, she decided to busy herself with household chores and check in on Ramla and her brother. Ramla slept peacefully in her crib, unaware of the sad state of her parents' marriage. Eva stroked her head and sang "Summertime", not as Sarah Vaughn sang it but as her own mother had when she was a child. She settled into the rocker watching the rise and fall of the tiny breaths, humming and losing herself in melancholy.

—

The alarm clock jangled Davis awake. He had slept through the night after tying one on the day before, his mind was sick because he had to find somewhere to live. He glanced over at Eva's side of the bed and noticed she wasn't there. He sat up to an awful hangover. His saliva was thick and a dull ache settled just above his eyes. He got up, showered and put down his first beer, tossing the can in the trash as he saw Eva make her way downstairs.

"Where were you?"

"What do you care? You were so drunk that you slept clean through the night. I am sick of living this type of life with you Davis."

He ignored her comments and walked out the door. Part of him hated her, yet another part lusted after her. It had been months since they had sex and he was feeling it. Eva was tired of Davis wanting to make love, if you could call it that, after he drank. It was mechanical, heartless. He would wake up, roll over, spread her legs, and ride her until he was satisfied. There was no tenderness or passion, only the thrusting of his hips, sometimes rhythmical and sometimes not depending on how drunk he was.

There were the phone calls during the day, sometimes at night, and always from a woman asking for Davis. When Eva questioned the caller, she would hang up. Eva was no fool. Of course he was cheating on her. What was there to do? The children were young, yes, but she already felt like a single parent. She didn't need Davis; he was dead weight to her. She had to cut him loose.

—

Satan observed Davis and Eva's misery, and delighted in their shambles. From the darkness, he appeared before the angels as a snake, twisting and writhing his message. Then a handsome man rose from the form of the snake—an incredibly handsome man--well-dressed, well-scented, aglow with beautiful hair and attractive features. A prideful man. He would establish again with Peter and the angels his cunning, his ability to deceive, his power to appear as one of the most beautiful creatures on earth. In the next instant, he changed back to the deadly asp.

Satan coiled around Peter and whispered, "Angels, the parents are failing. Watch and see what comes next. Insanity!"

Peter stood his ground, but could feel Satan's squeeze. "Let go of me, Satan! You have no control over me!"

Satan hissed and waved his forked tongue at Peter and materialized in Ramla's bed.

"What a sweet child," he mocked.

After that he appeared in the little boy's room, set on carrying out his evil plan. Slithering up into the crib, he wrapped himself around the sleeping boy's neck. He clung and tightened as the child startled. The small limbs thrashed and fought him, the throat choked. When silence fell over the last breath Satan vanished and only whispered his adieu, "Insanity!"

—

While preparing dinner, Eva thought she heard her son's cry. It sounded unusual. She went feet flying to his bedroom and plucked him from his crib. His body hung limp and was clammy. She screamed, "Somebody help me!"

No adult was in the house, and the neighbors lived too far to hear her. She kept her hold on him and gently shook him, in hopes that he would revive. She ran for the phone and heard the front door open. It was Davis. She yelled down to him, "Call the police. Something is wrong with Clay."

Davis, sober, bounded the stairs to them. Upon seeing them, he jabbed 911 into the phone.

Davis tried to administer cardiopulmonary resuscitation but his mind was too confused to remember the proper steps. In his heart, he knew the child was dead. The paramedics arrived and tried to stimulate the child but it was no use. In less than an hour, he was officially pronounced dead at the hospital.

Eva cried and wouldn't allow anyone to comfort her. Inwardly, Davis blamed her for the death of his only son. Their marriage got even worse after the funeral. They stopped speaking to one another. Soon Eva began to hate Davis and wanted nothing to do with him, she blamed him for her sons death.

One day, while standing in front of the mirror, Eva gazed at her floral dress. Her choice in clothing was beginning to change. She had abandoned her religion and; subconsciously favoring a look of power. She took a look into her closet and decided to wear slacks. Eva's appearance was strong and dominant. After smoothing her hair, she grabbed her cigarettes and placed one in her mouth. She lit it with a finesse that took years to achieve. She shot the mirror a brooding look and breathed curls of smoke in and out without ever touching the cigarette. Tonight, she was going out.

"Years had passed and Ramla had become a beautiful young teenager with more responsibilities added to her daily chores, be sure to watch your cousin. He has been through a lot since your aunt sister Rita died, be patient with him. Little Clay will be staying until he graduate's from high school. I'll be home later."

"Yes, Momma."

Eva grabbed a beer out of the icebox and took three aspirin. She had a flippin' headache, one that felt as if it were slowly driving her insane. She heard constant voices pounding against her skull, from the inside out. From sun-up to sundown, she played host to a multitude of conversations in her head.

After making sure that her daughter and nephew had something to eat, Eva headed toward town. The club was a lesbian bar. Eva walked in and sauntered over to the bar. She struck a conversation with a lady and traced her curves. The smoky haze hung thick in the air as the music pulsed a monotonous beat; one that stimulated lust in Eva.

The idea of being with another woman was intoxicating. Her new, more masculine look ensured that she would be the one to take control. The only time she felt out of control these days was when she listened to the voices in her head.

"Eva, God wants you to be with this woman. If you live with this woman, God will give you riches beyond compare. Ramla will also be blessed from this union and become extremely wealthy. You will always be taken care of."

Eva believed and was overcome with joy. She would be rich, and God would bless her many times over. Eva thanked the singular voice each time she heard it.

"You're welcome," it murmured.

—

Ramla and her best friend Kathy from school noticed Eva's transformation from an attractive and feminine woman to that of a masculine troll. Ramla felt she was losing the essence of her mother. She later learned just how much of her mother she was losing to the voices in her head. Ramla came home from school one day and found her mother sitting in the living room on the lap of a strange woman. She knew the woman was different, unlike anyone she had met. Ramla gazed around the room and noticed what could only be some of the woman's things moved into their home. Black plastic bags were stacked high near the sofa, full of clothes. Two nightstands and a lamp crowded the hallway that led to the kitchen. She noticed a roach crawling near her bags and smelled dirty undergarments.

"Ramla, this is Bernadette. She is going to be living with us now. If you aren't in agreement with it, pray the serenity prayer. Believe me when I tell you, this is a situation that you cannot change."

The statement was short and direct. There was no mistaking the relationship or the intent. Ramla stared at Bernadette and watched her mother light her cigarette in a weird and seductive manner. Eva walked over to Ramla and reached for her right hand, placing it in her jacket pocket. To Ramla's surprise she felt a gun. Ramla was afraid and starting shaking. She understood without asking that she was never to challenge her mother again. Eva looked into Ramla's eyes and pulled it out and said, "If anyone tries to break up Bernadette and me, I will have to kill them."

Home would be very different now. Shortly after breaking the news to Ramla, Eva began to excitedly tell her daughter of the riches she would inherit if she would flow with her plans. She believed God spoke to her and told her it was so. Ramla was confused and wondered why God would bless a lesbian affair when the Bible explicitly condemned it. She took an immediate dislike to Bernadette and didn't care for her mother's odd behavior—a poor imitation of a man.

Home life became difficult. Bernadette and her mother constantly fought. Eva grew weary of the bickering and took swift action on her lover. She wasted no time asserting her dominance by pushing Bernadette around and calling her condescending names. Bernadette complied and submitted, just the way Eva wanted.

"This woman is lucky to be with you, Eva. God is going to shower you with happiness and riches. There will be more women that will believe and join your calling."

The voices were unrelenting. From the time her head hit the pillow at night until she woke the next morning. The chatter grew more frequent and more explicit. She felt as if she was insane.

"Insanity!"

three

The angels gathered together. They knew that Satan would continue to test Ramla's faith. Slowly, he was tearing away her emotional and spiritual foundation. He had effortlessly lured her parents into hatred, addiction, extramarital affairs, decadent lifestyles and insanity. The angels waited, somber and anxious.

"Angels.....Ramla is next."

Satan began to place his plan into motion. Sammael would be his weapon to entice Ramla. He was certain that his strategy would keep Ramla from her destiny. He retreated to the shadows to observe Ramla and Sammael.

"Without a parent to guide them, young adults will surely fall into the temptation of the flesh," he sneered.

—

As a result of her mother's stormy relationships and mind attacks, Ramla's life became more uncertain. She longed for comfort and stability. She needed someone to understand and help her digest the many changes that were transpiring in her young life. Her hormones were going wild, and little did she suspect that demons were on assignment within her. She was at an awkward age, not yet grown but having to function as a young woman. She was unsure, like a colt taking its first steps. Ramla was moving tentatively toward womanhood. She began to have cravings for the attention of the opposite sex. When Ramla was twelve, Eva sent her off to Georgia to spend time with her sister and brother-in-law.

"Fresh country air will do you a bit of good Ramla. Besides I need a break from you."

Ramla knew there was nothing she could say to change her mother's mind.

"Momma, when do I leave?"

"Just as soon as your bum of a father sends the money for your plane ticket. Ramla, why do you have that crazy look on your face? Fix your face girl."

"My stomach hurts," she complained. "And I don't want to leave you."

"Oh girl, shut up and start packing. I don't want to hear that baby talk. It's time for you to grow up and start taking on some responsibilities."

Two days later Ramla sat alone on American Eagle Flight #247 en route to Lawrenceville, Georgia via Atlanta. Her mother told her that Aunt Mae would drive forty-five minutes to pick her up there.

"I sure hope Aunt Mae is on time. Will she know me when she sees me? Where should I wait for her? What will I do if she doesn't come?" Her mind raced and she sat up straighter and peered out the window. The small plane touched down and taxied to a stop. She thought she could actually see Aunt Mae waving. From her seat Ramla waved back, not sure if Aunt Mae could see her. Her aunt was beautiful. It felt good to her to see a woman all dressed up.

As she walked down the steps and landed her feet on Georgia's pavement, her soul felt steady, and she took a deep breath. Aunt Mae ran towards Ramla and hugged her.

"I'm so excited to see you Ramla. How have you been? Gosh, you sure have grown up since the last time I saw you. So answer my question sweetheart…How have you been doing?"

"Just fine Ma'am… I guess."

"You guess? What do you mean?" Aunt Mae's eyebrow went up and she leaned over to whisper in Ramla's ear, "I heard about your Momma's new lifestyle. I guess that's enough to make any young girl feel wacky and totally confused. Your momma's done lost her mind. You just pick up your chin from off this here ground and leave your cares behind. We're going to have a good time this summer. Every Sunday we go to church, you will love it. We have the best youth pastor in Georgia. Do you remember your cousin Alice? You two will get along just fine, seeing that the both of you are the same age and all. I'm going to let you know right now… in my house young folks earn their keep. We work poor Alice until her legs are about to fall off," Aunt Mae said as she laughed. "Ramla, I'm just kidding. Don't be so serious girl. Loosen up. Country life is much easier on the brain than all that city hustle and bustle."

Aunt Mae drove up to the house and Alice ran out to meet them, dust flying everywhere. She was bursting with excitement at the sight of her cousin who'd visit her for the entire summer.

"Come on Ramla, let's put your clothes away!"

Alice almost pulled Ramla's arm off as she dragged her into her bedroom, desperate to show off her new canopy bed.

"Look what my mother and daddy brought me for my birthday," Alice said proudly.

She knew that Ramla's mother could never afford such a bed for her. Alice heard some of the gossip about Ramla's home life, and considered building up her own confidence at Ramla's expense.

"So, tell me about your bedroom. Does it look like this?"

"No, not at all," Ramla replied.

"Hmm, what type of bed do you have??

"I share a bunk bed with my younger cousin."

"Yikes! Are you serious? Girl you need some excitement in your life. That's alright. Before this summer is over you will feel like you're on top of the world. Have you ever seen porn?"

"Porn, what is that?"

"You come from the city and you mean to tell me you don't know what porn is? You need to wise up Ramla."

Ramla was feeling not so comfortable in her Aunt Mae's home. She knew it was important to toughen up. If she remained the soft, sweet child that got off of that plane, the shark in her cousin would eat her alive.

Uncle Raymond yelled upstairs twice for the girls to come down for dinner.

"I am not going to call you girls another time. If you miss dinner, that will be on you. Don't come crying and begging for dinner later tonight when it's time to clean the stores."

"Clean the stores. What stores?"

"Momma didn't tell you? That is what we do. It's the family business. Don't worry. I know how to make the time go by fast. Come on let's go eat."

Uncle Raymond was the get-up-and-go type. He had inventions that dated back to 1960. Early in the seventy's he established the family's cleaning business.

"Whoa! Aunt Mae, this food sure smells good!" Ramla's nose took one good whiff of the sweet potato pie, cornbread stuffing, string beans, and juicy roast beef and it sent her stomach to clapping.

After dinner Aunt May rushed the girls off to bed.

"You girls only have a few hours to sleep before we go to work," she said.

"Oh Ramla, you just got fattened for the kill," chuckled Alice.

Ramla couldn't help but laugh. "I know Alice. I felt that."

"You girls go to sleep now, you hear," Aunt May yelled.

"Is work exciting?" Ramla asked, a little afraid of stepping on new ground. "My Dad used to say that he hated his job. That made me not want to work."

"Oh Ramla, what does your dad know? He sounded like the lazy type and I heard, he slept with a bottle of liquor under his pillow when he stopped sleeping with your momma."

"Alice, don't talk about my daddy like that."

"Okay. Don't be so doggone sensitive."

"I said, you girls better go to sleep in there, and stop all of that yapping," yelled Aunt Mae.

The girls rolled over, unaware that Ramla's demon was lurking around the house, waiting for his moment.

Next morning Aunt Mae called to them, "Get up girls. It's time to go…your daddy and uncle Joe aren't going to wait forever for you two to get dressed, so hurry up. You can drink your juice in the car."

The girls jumped out of bed, rubbed their eyes and slipped into their jeans. They raced down the hallway, grabbed their juice, and flew out the front door with Aunt Mae on their heels.

"Aunt Mae said that I could use the money I make to buy a new dress for church, didn't you Aunt Mae? I'm going to work real hard because I want a pretty lavender dress to wear for summertime."

"You girls buckle up your seatbelts. We are running late," Uncle Raymond admonished from the driver's seat.

The big Buick sped off. Ramla and Alice both had small frames that bounced up and down with every pot hole in the road.

"Raymond, when was the last time you had those shocks looked at? These girls are hitting the roof trying to stay in their seats.

"Mae, when you start working full-time, then you can complain about this car. Until then sit back and relax, those girls are fine.

As soon as the car slowed down in the parking lot Alice poked Ramla's side and yelled, "Come on girl. I have to use the bathroom."

"Me too."

Alice ran ahead of Ramla because she knew exactly where she was going, screaming, "This way... hurry. Me first., me first!"

"No, please let me go first. I have to go bad," Ramla pleaded holding on to the sides of her jeans.

Both pulled their jeans and panties down at the same time. Alice jumped on the toilet, and by the look on her face she dared Ramla to say another word. Ramla bent over with her knees tightly pinned together, trying with all of her muscles to hold it in. "Shoot, hurry up. I'm about to pee on myself."

Alice jumped off of the toilet, flushed it and moved out of her way.

"Whoa, relief," sighed Ramla. She took a deep breath and was overjoyed that she made it just in time.

"Alice what are you doing, what's in there?" Ramla asked.

"Hush, be quiet... this is what I call the secret stash."

Alice had reached to the back of the bathroom cabinet and pulled out several magazines with half-naked women on the front. The girls didn't know that legions of demons had gathered in the bathroom and were elated at the beginning of their plan to enter Ramla's soul.

—

"It's just a matter of time before we have another house to enter. Many bodies house demons." The head demon reminded them to stay far from the blood of Jesus. "If you hear someone talk about the power of the blood, get out of there before they recognize you and cast you out. Know that they have authority, in the name of Jesus, to use the power of the blood against you. If you are detected and they approach the human that houses you, be gentle and talk in a sweet, non-assuming voice. This behavior works most of the time because some Christians don't know how to balance out the gift of mercy. They will end up feeling sorry for the person and walk away, right at the point of deliverance. Believe me when I tell you, you don't want deliverance to take place. If it does, you will end up in dry, dark places you blood sucking demons. It is your duty to keep yourself safe; there is a long line of demons waiting for a body to consume. They wait on so-called believers to throw their hands up and give into the flesh. Foolish and unlearned Christians do not understand that we can get seven more demons to possess the human body once they decide to turn back."

—

"Look Ramla, this is what I was telling you earlier about porn."

"Nasty," whispered Ramla. "What are they doing? They are upside down. Oh, my gosh!"

The girls jumped at the sound of Aunt Mae pulling on the door knob. Ramla fell down, scared that they had been caught.

"Hold on Momma, we are just finishing up. Boy, it's a good thing I locked the door behind us," whispered Alice. "Momma would kill me if she knew how much I loved porn."

"You love it. Why?"

"I do because it makes me feel good."

"Feel good? No way. It's nasty. Yuck."

"Come on Ramla, Momma is going to get suspicious."

—

"Demon of lust, this is your chance to enter. Wait until Ramla falls to sleep. Her mind will be resting, and it has not been covered by the blood of Jesus. There is no one to fight against our plan. Go in during her sleep. If you fail, Satan will be angry and you may never be given the opportunity to inhabit another soul. Remember, several others are assigned to enter during the idle times of Ramla's mind. That is when we get to play. Many minds have become our playground."

—

Night after night Alice subjected Ramla to porn until her consciousness was comfortable with the sight of it. During this time demons penetrated her mind and body and dwelled there.

Peter watched this and was furious with Satan. He called to the angel of destiny.

"This is war. I can't just sit around and watch Satan infiltrate this innocent child's mind. This is absurd. There is no way heaven would allow this to happen. Where is Michael the arch angel? It's time to fight. I mean it. This is war!"

"Calm down Peter. You aren't calling the shots. Your understanding is minimal. Where sin abounds, grace abounds even more. I know the facts that you are seeing. The reality of sin is devastating and it hurts. We see it over and over again. Be patient. God will make a way of escape for His own children. He loves Ramla. Just step back and try to hold your composure."

"He will make a way if Ramla willingly follows him. Am I correct?" asked Peter.

"Yes, you are correct Peter."

"How will she follow God after going through a period of being brainwashed by Satan and his demons? None of this is fair. Where is the justice in all of it?"

"Remember the word faith, Peter? You must believe against all odds and listen to what your heart is saying. Just believe. You have to see past what surrounds Ramla and have faith that one day she will escape the onslaught of the enemy. Humans have suffered in this manner ever since the fall of mankind. Know that our redeemer is Yeshua. Find it in your heart to trust him."

"I do trust him but I saw many enter into hell on this morning."

"Yes, many die and go into hell Peter. That is their choice. They have chosen to take the path that is wide."

"Well, there's no guarantee that Ramla will choose life. What if she remains ignorant to the truth and doesn't steer clear of the path that so many others have fallen onto?"

"Peter, only God truly knows if she is going to make it or not, for he is the Alpha and the Omega. Only God knows. Our job is to pray and believe. You are called to observe, for there is a lesson in this assignment that will change you forever."

Peter prayed with a burning desire to learn all that God intended for him to learn. He tried earnestly to embrace the power and strength of what was being taught to him, the words of the Almighty. His faith had not yet moved beyond his feelings, sight, and sound. He made up in his mind not to allow the cares of life to hinder him from winning this time. He returned to the Pond of Contemplation and as he looked into Ramla's life, he saw that many days had passed and the summer was ending. Ramla was on her way back home from Georgia.

—

As she climbed out of the cab she turned to pay the cab driver. She noticed him looking at her, not as a young teenager, but as an older woman. This brought about the same feelings that she had become familiar with while staying in Georgia. She smiled back at him, paid the fare, grabbed her suitcase, and ran in the house.

"Momma, I'm home!"

"Good. Did you enjoy your summer?"

"Sure did! I had a great time with Aunt Mae, Alice, and Uncle Raymond."

"Great! Ramla, you are going to sleep in the basement from now on."

"Momma, the basement? Why?"

"Because I said so. You'll have much more room. Besides you are getting older and those boobs are started to stick out, you ain't a little girl anymore. You are too old now to sleep in the same room with your little cousin. Your period will be coming on soon, so go on and move your things to the basement."

Ramla had become close to Alice, so she tip-toed into the family room and called her long distance.

"Alice, guess what? My mother is making me sleep in the basement. Can you believe that? She is using this dumb excuse that I am getting too old to sleep in the same room with my cousin, but I know the deal. She doesn't want me to hear her and Bernadette making those crazy noises. I didn't understand before, but I do now."

Laughing out loud, Alice agreed with Ramla and said, "Girl, your mother is crazy. Just hang in there. I have to go. Your momma would kill us if she knew we were talking long distance without permission."

"Okay. I'll write to you instead."

"Sure, I look forward to seeing you next summer Ramla. And do me a favor, find yourself a boyfriend."

Ramla hung up the phone and began moving her things into the basement. She felt as if someone was watching her. It was Bernadette.

"Hey, did you have a good time in Georgia?"

"Yes Ma'am I did."

"I heard you worked while you were there. Did you make any real money??

"I made enough to buy myself some dresses for church."

"Church? Honey, ain't nobody taking you to church around here. The only church you will attend is the one your momma is preparing for her new calling. She's gonna be rich one day."

" Ms. Bernie, do you really believe that?"

"Yes I do. Don't you?"

"Well, I just don't know. Momma said she is gonna have more wives. Doesn't that make you feel a little funny? I mean, aren't you jealous of that idea?"

"Baby girl, it's not an idea. It's what God told her."

"It's what Satan told her," Ramla said under her breath.

"What did you say girl?"

"Oh nothing." Ramla hung her shoulders low, afraid of a backlash from her.

"You'd better watch that mouth, Miss Sassy. If God said it, then it's so. No need for me to worry about the words of a prophet."

Ramla wondered to herself, "What is a prophet?"

Bernie busied herself in the basement as Ramla finished unpacking and got ready for the first day of school.

"My friend Carmen invited me to go out with her. Is that okay with you?"

"Fine. Your mother has to work all weekend and I'm sure she won't mind. Just be careful."

Ramla neatly placed all of her clothes in the drawers. She decided to be responsible for her own peace. Her experience in Georgia made her feel mature and all grown up. Besides, she just turned sixteen, and felt her new teenage status coming on.

Later that month at a social function for one of her classmates, Ramla detected her reflection in the eyes of a young man she hadn't seen before. His eyes were rich and dark, matching his intensity. Ramla wasn't used to attention from boys. She enjoyed the sidelong glances. She found the courage to approach him and introduced herself.

To Sammael, she was the most attractive girl he had ever seen. And, being a teenage boy, he was determined to have her. Ramla was smitten with Sammael as well. Everything about him aroused her: his voice, his eyes, his hands. She longed to kiss his full lips. As they talked and got to know each other a bit better, Sammael could contain himself no longer. He pulled Ramla close and kissed her. Ramla's head began to swim as she felt his hands caress her breasts. He stopped long enough to talk her into leaving the party so they could go down the street to his house. Sammael's mother was at work and he was sure that she wouldn't be coming in anytime soon.

He took Ramla's hand and led her to his home where he kissed her and offered her a soda and a slice of apple pie just for the heck of it. She accepted. His mind was on one thing and he was set on getting it. After pie and soda, he kissed her again and guided her to his bedroom.

Ramla could tell that Sammael had sex before. He took her to his bed, his hands leaning her back and expertly undressing her while they kissed. She was completely naked and watched him unbutton his jeans and climb in bed next to her. She was unsure of what to expect and began to get scared.

Sammael whispered, "Relax."

He placed himself inside of her. She whimpered from the pain. He took her virginity. When he was done, they rested and said nothing. Then, without warning, Sammael climbed back on top of Ramla and began to do it again. Ramla became afraid when she looked down and noticed blood on the sheets.

"See. It's better the second time around," he whispered oblivious to the tear that ran down her cheek. She had become uncomfortable with the decision she allowed him to make for her. Sammael's appetite for sex got bigger and became more savage. She was frightened and begged him to stop, but he ignored her. He was hurting her, brutally thrusting deeper and deeper inside her, until he was gratified again.

"You better go now. My mother will be home soon. I'll walk you home if you want."

"No, I will walk home by myself."

Fearing a front-door encounter with Sammael's mother, she climbed out his bedroom window and walked home. She felt like a piece of trash. Everyone in her house was asleep. Ramla silently went upstairs and changed into her nightclothes. She got up into her bed and listened to the crickets chirp outside her window. She was sore and traumatized by her first sexual experience. She wished this was something she could discuss with her mother. But she knew better.

—

"Well, well, well angels. Ramla is a woman now," Satan taunted.

"She will learn from this experience. One encounter doesn't mean she will suffer lifelong consequences," reasoned the angel of destiny.

"Satan, why did you make the boy take her twice? You accomplished your goal the first time," Peter asked

Satan roared an evil laugh and reveled in the disturbed silence of the angels. He turned himself into the handsome image of Sammael and strutted around them with his chest sticking out. Peter looked over at the angel of destiny echoing his amazement at the transformation.

"Angels, the rabbit has died!" Satan hissed.

—

Ramla was vomiting every morning for a week when her mother took her in for examination. They waited now for the doctor to return. Eva's head was in her hands.

"Are you sure?" she asked.

"Yes ma'am. The blood test confirms the pregnancy."

Ramla sat on the table looking down. She was petrified of being pregnant. She never felt more alone than she did at that moment. She knew she had to tell everyone in her life. One thing she knew for sure, she wouldn't be able to stay for long with her mother, not as long as she was taking in female lovers.

"Why in the world didn't you tell me you wanted sex? I could have gotten your behind on some birth control pills."

"I don't know Momma."

"Does that boy know he's gonna be a daddy?"

"No, I'll tell him tonight."

"No, I'll tell his Momma tonight so we can make sure he makes an honest woman out of you."

Eva considered the options. Either way, Ramla was in a difficult place.

"Eva, Ramla has been chosen. She is to carry that baby and become a mother. God chose her. She will give you riches beyond your dreams."

Eva trusted the voice. Ramla told Eva that she had seen Sammael in the grocery store and she seemed to be approachable. Eva decided to pay a visit to the boy's mother and tell them about the pregnancy.

"Come child, it's time to face the music."

Ramla was mortified that her mother was dragging her to Sammael's home to tell his mother about the baby. And, to make things worse, she was wearing a man's suit, determined to appear manly for whatever reason.

"Wasn't her short haircut enough like a man's to prove her make-believe manhood" Ramla thought.

"Eva, let me come with you and Ramla," Bernadette asked.

"No Bernie, you are to stay and tend to this house. Now make sure dinner is ready when we get back." Eva gave Bernie a stern look reasserting the power she had over her.

Ramla and Eva walked to Sammael's house, not saying a word. They reached their destination and walked up the driveway. Eva rapped her knuckles on the door and waited. A pleasant looking woman answered and smiled at them both.

"May I help you?"

"Yes, you may. My name is Eva and I am Ramla's mother, your son has been dating my daughter for three months and she is pregnant. You do have a son named Sammael.

"Why, yes I do. Is there a problem here?"

The woman looked concerned.

"We'll tell you all about it. Can we come in?"

Eva was in no mood to be polite.

"Certainly, right this way."

The woman motioned for them to come in and led them into the living room. An overstuffed floral print sofa brightened the room. The carpet looked new and the fragrance of fresh flowers filled the room. What looked to be tulips and peonies stood bright and fresh in a large vase on the coffee table.

"May I get you a cup of coffee or tea?"

"No, we're fine."

Eva plopped herself on the couch and Ramla sat cautiously beside her, looking down.

"Sammael! Come here, please."

She turned her attention back to Eva and Ramla, and extended her hand.

"My name is Sandra Cox. And you are?"

"My name is Eva and this here is my daughter, Ramla. She is already well acquainted with your son," Eva said sarcastically.

Sammael walked into the living room and appeared as if he had been ambushed. He looked at Ramla with questioning eyes and received no answers from her.

"Alright Eva, you have our attention. What is it that you came over here to tell us?" Sandra asked.

"Mrs. Cox, your son got my daughter pregnant. I don't know how long they have been sexually active, but I can tell you it didn't happen in my home. My daughter is sixteen years old, and I would like to know what you are going to do about it."

Sandra Cox turned to her son and asked him for the truth.

"Did you get this girl pregnant? Boy, you better tell me the truth!"

"We slept together, but she never said anything about being pregnant. I swear."

Looking at the three women in the room, he knew he wasn't likely to win this battle.

"Eva and Ramla, I apologize for my son. He sometimes has a difficult time keeping his zipper up, just like his daddy."

"Eva, let me digest this information and see what we can do to help in this situation. I'm not sure having these kids marry is the answer. May I contact you in a few days to discuss again?"

"Sure, you can call me at home. My telephone number is 222 864-3476."

Eva stood up and grabbed her crotch as if some appendage had appeared overnight and was in need of adjustment. She then reached out for Ramla's hand and out the door they went. Again, no words were spoken on the way home. Ramla knew that her mother would be in a foul mood.

As they walked into the front door, Bernadette announced that Davis had called and left a message for Ramla. He wanted to pick her up for a visit. Ramla looked at her mother with pleading eyes. All she wanted to do is go to her bedroom and stay there forever. She didn't want to talk to anyone about her pregnancy.

"Girl, don't give me that look. When your Daddy picks you up, you are going to tell him about your belly that's about to swell."

Eva dropped in her seat at the table and began scooping food onto her plate that Bernadette had fixed for them. Ramla sat down and ate in silence.

Eva chatted away as her mood suddenly shifted, "Child, this baby is going to be a blessing. God said so. Hallelujah!"

"That's right. Ramla's baby will be the second coming of Jesus. Just think Eva. Your own baby girl will carry Jesus. God will bestow all kinds of gifts and fortunes. Hallelujah!" sang an ecstatic Bernadette.

Satan murmured into Eva's ear.

"Bernie, Momma needs to go out and celebrate. Go put on a pretty dress and off we will go."

Ramla noticed that Eva called her Bernie when she was in a good mood. She was disgusted by their relationship and didn't want to live with her child in her mother's house.

four

Ramla sat in the living room while waiting for her father to arrive. She felt queasy, and didn't know if it was the pregnancy or if she was filled with dread at the thought of telling him about the baby. Maybe it was both. Her thoughts were interrupted by the familiar slam of her father's car door. She watched him walk up the sidewalk, and smiled. To her, he was the most handsome father in the world. She hated that her parents divorced, and longed for them to get back together so that things would return to normal. She wanted to see her mother back in black elegant dresses, acting more herself.

"Hello, Princess. How's my baby girl?" Davis called out through the screen door.

"Daddy, I'm okay. I've missed you so much."

Ramla grabbed him around his middle and hugged him tight. She was fighting to hold back the tears that rushed forward at the comfort of her daddy's embrace. She felt protected for the first time in months. Together they walked to his car and small-talked until they reached his house. She always enjoyed visiting with her father and hearing about his work, friends, and his side of the family.

Things felt normal with him. She also liked seeing her stepmother, Jessica. She was a kind woman who looked the other way when Davis came home drunk or caroused with other women. She loved his children, and was the type of person that Ramla felt she could talk to.

"Jess, we're home. Come see how much Ramla has grown."

Davis was awfully proud of his little girl and couldn't believe how she was growing up so fast, right before his eyes.

"Ramla, you're becoming a beautiful young woman," Jessica announced.

Davis settled himself on the floor, leaning against the seat of the couch. Ramla joined him as Jessica brought him a beer. Davis downed it and asked for another. In no time, she had brought him three beers and a straight glass of Jack Daniel..

"Daddy, please slow down. Three beers along with that drink is way too much. Don't go messing up your mind and body with all of that alcohol. Daddy, there is something I have to tell you."

Ramla's eyes welled with tears as she lowered her head in shame. She couldn't bear to see the disappointment in her father's eyes. She had learned from an early age that the best time to tell her father bad news was when he was under the influence of alcohol, he would use laughter to reject disappointment.

"What is it, Princess?"

"I met a boy....and, well....I'm pregnant."

"Jess, bring me another beer!"

Davis was upset and angry. His little girl was only sixteen.

"How far along are you?"

"Three months or so."

Davis nodded and mumbled that things would be okay. He continued to drink and for two hours and he demanded Ramla explain to him every detail that led up to her becoming pregnant. Davis also wanted to know Sammael's address. Ramla could tell her father was becoming inebriated. He repositioned himself on the floor and passed out. As Ramla listened to his deep rhythmical breathing, she became sleepy. She got up and went into the guest bedroom where she too fell asleep.

Davis slept for awhile. When he awoke he noticed that Ramla left the living room. He got up and peeked into the bedroom where she napped. He couldn't believe she was pregnant. He watched her. Ramla was a beautiful girl and was voluptuous for her sixteen years. He felt himself begin to stiffen with excitement. He became enchanted with her breasts as she deeply inhaled. He sat on the side of the bed and lightly touched one of them. He felt the warmth and softness he craved. Davis gently pulled her legs apart and stared at her face to make sure she was still sleeping. She stirred a bit but returned to sleep. He unzipped his pants and cautiously removed her panties. He reached into his khakis and placed himself inside her, gradually and gently. Excitement overtook him. He began to thrust his hips. He hadn't felt this excited in years and couldn't control himself any longer. Suddenly, Ramla woke up to find her father on top of her, plunging himself into her. She screamed for him to stop but Davis didn't respond.

Jessica ran into the bedroom to see what the commotion was about and saw what was happening. She looked away and walked out; afraid to confront Davis. She went upstairs into their bedroom and shut the door. She paced and thought of what she could do. How could she get help for her husband? She was nervous and became sick on her stomach.

Davis held Ramla down and began grunting. Ramla knew there was no use in fighting him off. She would have to wait until he was finished before she could get away from him. She squeezed her eyes shut, and let the tears spill. It seemed like hours to Ramla, but lasted only a short period. He stayed on top of her for a few moments and at last rolled off. Davis was still drunk, struggling to stand up. He looked down at his daughter. She was crying hysterically.

"Get out of here, you whore! You open your legs for every Tom, Dick and Daddy, don't ya?"

Davis was disgusted. Ramla scrambled to her feet and put her underwear back on and ran all the way back home.

—

Satan chuckled at his conquest. Davis was weak when he drank, and his new wife was even weaker. He had to give it to himself -- rape, incest, shame, alcohol abuse, emotional abuse...check, check, check, check and check.

"This was too easy," mused Satan.

"Satan!"

"What? Who is shouting at me?"

"I am Peter, the angel of faith. You will fail, you despicable fiend. You will fail. I won't stand by and watch you destroy this young woman."

"That was the deal, Peter," Satan hissed.

"No! At this rate, Ramla has absolutely no one to introduce her to Jesus Christ, our Lord. She will not have a chance to overcome all of the evil you have thrown her way."

"Oh, what's a little evil between friends? I haven't even gotten started yet, boy!"

"What's the matter, Satan? Are you afraid if one person tells Ramla about God, that you would be out of her life completely? That's not very powerful of you."

Peter was angry and could hardly bear to watch Ramla endure the horrors that had happened. Satan stared at Peter and was silent for a few moments. He warily eyed the other angels and saw their determination to fight him. Setting up Ramla to fail seemed easy for him. He wanted a tougher challenge.

"Alright Peter, I do need a little contest. This is entirely too trouble-free. But, there are a few ground rules."

"Such as?"

"You can introduce people in her life to help with her faith, but it ultimately has to be her choice as to whether or not she decides to change her life. You can't inhabit her body or use your wisdom to guide her. She is in complete control, at all times."

"Oh, just like she was when her father raped her?"

Peter knew Satan wasn't playing fair.

"Take it or leave it, boy! I'm growing tired of you and your demands."

"I'll take it. Wait! Once she gives her heart to Jesus and invites the Holy Spirit in, he will bring comfort to her. That is written. Be prepared to see miracles, Satan! Be prepared!"

—

Ramla burst into her home and ran downstairs to her bedroom in the basement crying.

"Good Lord, child. What is the matter?" Eva wanted to know.

She followed after her daughter and found her sobbing on her bed. Ramla jumped up, dashed for the bathroom and heaved. She came back and told her mother what transpired. Eva stared at her daughter and became irritated. Ramla discerned that the voices were talking to her again. She couldn't keep up with her mother's irrational frame of mind.

"Ramla, God told me why you are distraught by your father's behavior."

Eva was convinced. She had heard the voice just moments before Ramla ran through the front door.

"Eva, Davis had his way with Ramla. She is very upset because, like you, she has discovered that she needs to be with a woman too. She likes you. Give her the privilege of being with you. That is why she is so upset.....she wants you, not Davis!"

Eva sat on the side of Ramla's bed and shared with her what the voice told her.

She touched her daughter's cheek and looked deep into her eyes.

"Sweetheart, Jehovah told me that you wanted me instead of Davis. It's all right. I understand what it's like to desire a woman."

She said it so straightforward that Ramla was stunned at what she heard.

"What?"

Eva leaned over and tried to kiss her daughter on the lips. Ramla pushed her away and ran to the other side of the room. Eva followed her and slapped her in the face. She kissed her on her lips. Ramla pushed her away again, moved over to her bed, crying as she pulled her knees up to her chest and curled up into a knot underneath the covers. She was confused and beside herself with sorrow. Eva sighed and left her alone. Ramla surely felt she was in hell. She sobbed for the loss of her purity, she longed for her innocence back.

She detected a smell in her room—a fragrance. She sat up. She breathed it in. It was sweet and comforting. Something in it made her feel reassured, at peace. She wondered if it was a figment of her imagination, if she was starting to sense things, just like her mother.

The guardian angels were standing at the foot of her bed watching over her. Their unseen presence provided her a pleasant respite. They were hoping that this was the moment she would cry out to God for help.

—

"Peter, come. Ramla will find her way to Jesus. We have to allow events in her life to occur as they must. God knew in the beginning of her life what would take place. The hearts of men are wicked; many children suffer because of them. Believe that she will overcome, just believe," said the angel of destiny.

"But why? Why does God want her to suffer?" Peter asked.

"He doesn't want her to suffer. God is angry too. He sees the wickedness of Ramla's parents, and the sickness in their minds. Unbeknownst to you, God wanted to destroy them both, but an old lady prayed for their souls years ago. God had grace on them. It is his desire that no man perish, but for all to come to him. Hopefully they will obey God and be an example of how powerful his love for us can be. Anyone in dire circumstances can overcome evil when the demons of darkness torment a soul. That is the lesson for Ramla and for mankind. Be joyful, Peter. God is leading the way."

"Praise Yeshua! Hallelujah!" exalted Peter.

—

Ramla roused from a deep but restless slumber. Yesterday's encounter with her father swirled in her head, "How could he? I hate him. Maybe it was me, what did I do to lead him on? No. No. It couldn't have been me. I love my dad, but not like that. My life is crazy...I trusted him. He is nothing but a drunk and a rapist. God where are you? I hate them both. Why was I ever born into this family? My mother is walking around looking like a man, and had the nerve to say you told her I wanted her. Well, at least I know for a fact she is not hearing from you, God. My life is a mess, a curse. I feel dirty. I must run away from here. Maybe Mrs. Cox will allow me to come and live with her and Sammael."

Ramla knew she couldn't continue to live with her mother much longer. Although she loved her dearly, she hated seeing and being trapped in a lifestyle that wasn't normal. She didn't know how to and no longer wanted to deal with the voices her mother kept hearing. Her mother's disposition was completely unpredictable and she wasn't making sense anymore. Ramla did not understand her mother's state, all she knew was, it was tearing her mind to pieces. This place wouldn't be a safe environment for her baby.

She got herself together and decided to go to Sammael's home to speak with his mother. She had liked her the minute they met even though it was under stressful circumstances.

Eva looked up from reading the paper and saw that Ramla was preparing to go out.

"Child, where are you off to?"

"I'm just going to take a long walk. I want to be alone for awhile," she lied. The last thing she wanted was her mother going with her. She had been so belligerent the first time they met Mrs. Cox, no wonder nothing came of the meeting. No wonder she never contacted them like she said she would. Eva took a long drag off her cigarette and watched her daughter closely. ---It's probably all of the commotion and upset from yesterday, she thought and decided to not question her anymore about it. ---Ramla was a good girl, in spite of what happened to her.

Ramla walked to Mrs. Cox's house, engrossed in her thoughts. Before she knew it, she was standing on the front porch, knocking on the door. Sandra Cox opened the door to find the shy girl who was carrying her grandchild. She couldn't help but feel for her. She had been in her same predicament many years ago.

She smiled and greeted Ramla, "Well, hello. Please come in, dear."

Ramla returned the smile and stepped inside the door as Mrs. Cox guided her to the living room and invited her to sit on the sofa.

"Would you care for a soda or juice?"

"No ma'am. I'm fine. I just wanted to talk to you."

"What about a sandwich?"

Ramla wasn't sure what to say but she needed to find out what the future held for her. It wasn't to live with either parent. Tears started down her face as her nervous hands gathered the pale green dress around her knees.

"Goodness, child, go ahead....I'm sure you're a little anxious about what is happening."

Ramla swallowed and pulled her bangs back and began to talk. She shared everything about her home life. She told about her mother's mental frailty and Bernie, and about how her father had raped her. She was spilling out her emotions and couldn't stop. She desperately needed someone to listen and offer help.

Mrs. Cox listened and made mental notes. The girl's abuse was much more than she could've imagined. She had noticed that Ramla's mother seemed unbalanced, but wasn't quite sure of the extent. She thought it was due to the upsetting discovery of her daughter's pregnancy.

"I'm here for you, Ramla. Please know that. I love my son very much, and I am concerned about thinking of the two of you are becoming parents before you are ready. I need to ask you a question, and be honest with me, alright?"

She needed to get to the bottom of things.

"Yes ma'am."

Ramla was taken aback and all of a sudden felt as if she shouldn't have shared as much as she had.

"Do you love my son?"

"Oh, yes ma'am! I really do!" I know we were wrong having sex, but we have spent a lot of time together talking and having fun.

Sandra smiled and nodded, but she had her reservations about them raising a child at such a young age. They were entirely too young. Besides, she knew her son. He was terrified and wasn't ready to commit.

"Ramla, I'm going to call Sammael in to sit down and talk about this, okay?"

"Yes ma'am"

"Sammael. Please come in here."

---What does she want now! This is nothing but a set-up. Momma expects me to slow down my life to take care of a baby. I still do not understand why Ramla didn't abort it. I'm going to be tied down with this mess.

"Pretend like you're listening," whispered a voice. "Act like you care because momma is going to have the last word no matter what you think. Do you really think she has your best interest at heart? Believe me, boy, she is going to make you pay for your father's mistakes. Do not trust your mother, Sammael, you belong to me."

Sammael shuffled into the living room and sat next to Ramla. He didn't utter a word.

"Sammael, Ramla....I think the two of you are much too young to marry. But, she is going to have your baby. I do believe she needs your support and direction through all of this. So, I have decided to invite Ramla to live with us. It only makes sense at this point. And, young man, you will assist her and take her to doctor appointments and so forth. You will be actively involved. Now, this doesn't mean that I'm allowing you two to freely have sex in my home. I'm going to ask you to respect my home, and honor my decision to help Ramla and my new grandchild. Do I make myself clear?"

"Yes mom," Sammael acknowledged. "Ramla, I will help you move in, if you like."

Ramla smiled and gratefully accepted. Mrs. Cox nodded her head in approval. Her son made a life-altering mistake, but she was proud of him nonetheless. He was a good looking child and his boyish looks were slowly giving way to the handsome features of a man. Now if she could get his character to match.

five

"Mom, I need to talk to you!"

A voice from the back of the house shouted, "I'm in here!"

Ramla walked into the den area and found Eva smoking a cigarette and watching television.

"What is it?" Eva asked as she continued watching the small screen.

"Mom, Mrs. Cox has asked me to move in with her and Sammael. And, I think it is a good idea."

She was a bit nervous when the words left her mouth but she didn't feel that her mother would put up a fight.

"Does that boy have a flippin' job?." I hope he plans on taking care of you.

Ramla watched her mother blow smoke rings in the air and said nothing. After a momentary silence, Eva turned to look at Ramla.

"Yes, you can go to live with them. That's probably the only way you can get him to be involved in the birth of this baby."

Ramla stood up and kissed her mother on the top of her head and walked to her room. She hastily packed her things and called Sammael to help her.

For the first time in years, Ramla's mind was at ease. As nervous and scared as she was to give birth and raise a baby, she was just as thankful to have someone like Mrs. Cox to talk with and rely on.

—

Satan kept a vigilant eye on the change of living arrangements. He was getting more incensed by the minute.

"I specifically inflicted severe emotional pain on Ramla. I didn't have a stranger to rape her, it was her own father. And, I put the lust in Eva's heart toward her daughter. I should've been able to cripple her self-confidence and destroy her esteem. The emotional and physical torment should have been sufficient enough to create a faulty set of character traits. She should be unbalanced enough to develop a diabolical bridge so that my demons will have a permanent entryway to control her decisions and ultimately destroy her destiny. Curse Ramla! Curse the angels! And curse heaven!"

Satan roared his contempt for all things good.

"Ramla, you will fail! I will crush your emotions and you will carry the seed of misery inside your belly! I will not give up!"

He stopped for a moment to recalculate his plan. Satan wanted to see Ramla break down. He wanted to prove a point to God. Satan shouted, "More is to come, Ramla! More is to come!"

—

Ramla finished packing her suitcase and Sammael lugged it upstairs, he thought to himself, "*this is the least that I can do, I have caused Ramla so much trouble.* She felt a sense of liberation, knowing that the moments in her mother's house were soon coming to an end. She remained in the living room, apprehensively waiting for Sammael to arrive. Finally, he ambled up the sidewalk onto the front porch. Her heart quivered each time she saw him; he was the best looking boy she'd ever seen. To look at him almost felt as if she was under some type of spell. Ramla unlocked the door and grinned.

"By mom I love you."

"Come and give me a hug Ramla. "You take care of my daughter Sammael."

"Hello. Thanks for coming over to help me ."

"No problem. Mom said that she would've come too but she had to leave for work," he replied, lifting her luggage as he headed out the door.

The young couple walked in silence for most of the way to his home, Sammael's home was only a few blocks down the street. She timidly stepped inside the house, feeling more like an imposing visitor than someone invited to take up residence. It seemed different when Mrs. Cox wasn't there. Sammael took her hand and escorted her to her new room. It was a neat room, just big enough for a twin bed and a dresser. He planted her suitcase on the floor and sat on the bed. She stood frozen, unsure of what to do. He patted the bed and motioned for her to sit down beside him. Ramla sat next to him feeling shy, intrigued, scared and exhilarated, all at the same time.

"You know, Mom won't be home from work until late tonight."

"Oh, that's okay."

Ramla wasn't quite sure what Sammael meant. He reached over and placed a kiss on her cheek then pulled back to gauge her reaction. It was a soft, sweet kiss. Ramla craved affection and expression of love. Slowly, she leaned over and kissed him in return, and then turned away.

"Remember what your mom said... no hanky, panky. Please, I want to follow her rules. She might come home earlier than you think," Ramla warned him.

"No. I don't expect her home until the dead of night. I promise."

He caressed her face and softly kissed her lips. She gave in to his kiss and became entranced. She didn't need to be afraid of being with him; after all, he would soon be her husband. Sammael liked how daring and exciting it felt to be doing the forbidden with his girlfriend in his mother's home.

"I'm glad you liked it. I think this arrangement is going to work out great"

"What do you mean by that?"

"You're my woman now. I need a lot of sex. You're already pregnant, so it won't matter how much we do it."

"What about your mother? You can't expect me to just be with you at the drop of a hat when your mom isn't around, she replied anxiously.

"Relax, I'll sneak into your room when I want it and she'll never know."

Ramla put her clothes back on, contemplating.

—

Satan witnessed Ramla's first night at Sammael's house.

"Another seed of misery, Ramla. Another seed!" he boasted.

"Peter, I can almost see your question. Ask it, " the angel of destiny invited.

"How will she ever break free from this sin?"

"Peter, we have discussed this many times. Understand that the blood of Jesus can wash away her sins once she turns her heart from evil and repents. He is faithful to wash her clean through and through, whiter than the purest snow. Without spot or blemish, Ramla will be able to present herself to Jesus, a new bride washed in the blood. Just believe."

—

The next morning, Ramla woke up and looked around the unfamiliar room. She quickly remembered that she moved into Mrs. Cox's home. Then guilt hit her because of her disobedience to the rules. She sat up in bed and glanced at the clock. It was 7:30, relatively late for her. She showered and straightened her room. She wandered into the living room and found Mrs. Cox reading the paper and sipping a cup of tea.

Mrs. Cox looked up to see Ramla in the doorway. "Good morning, dear."

"Good morning, ma'am," Ramla softly replied.

"Now, now, we'll have none of that. Call me Ms. Sandra, sweetheart. You're carrying my grandbaby, so we're family now."

Ramla embraced the warmth and grinned. She appreciated being there, being invited to be there and make a home with them. Ms. Sandra was always pleasant and cheerful. Ramla wanted to be the same.

"Ms. Sandra, may I ask you a question?"

"Certainly, what is it?"

"You are so….so nice and at peace….how do you do that?"

Ramla struggled with her words, but finally managed to ask her what she longed to have in her own life.

Ms. Sandra looked at Ramla and smiled.

"Child, come into the kitchen. I'll make you a cup of tea and try to explain it the best way I can." She placed a steaming cup of tea in front of Ramla and sat across from her. "Do you know Jesus? Do you know God's love?"

Ramla was puzzled. She had gone to church with her Aunt Mae and cousin, but it felt like a long time ago. Since her parents divorced and her mother became a lesbian, God and the Bible were not as important to her as they once were. They talked all afternoon and didn't realize how many hours had passed.

"Goodness, look at the time. Ramla, would you like to go to church with me now?"

"I, I don't know...."

Ramla wanted to experience the peace that Sandra had, but didn't feel comfortable just yet in going to church. She was ashamed of her troubled life and didn't feel worthy enough to go. Sandra understood.

"Ramla, Mark 2:17 says, *It is not the healthy who need a doctor, but the sick. I have not come to call the righteous, but sinners.*

Ramla looked at Sandra, searching her face for explanation.

"Child, that scripture is from the Holy Bible. What it means is that church, Jesus and God are for those that are struggling and lost, not for those who have all the answers. They are here to help you, sweetheart." Ms. Sandra's eyes welled with tears as she hugged Ramla. "I'll tell you what, when you feel like you're ready to go to church with me, let me know. In the meantime, I'll keep asking you from time to time."

Ramla thanked her over and over again. She was glad there was no pressure. She felt a little strange, as if Ms. Sandra's words had come alive and brought her peace. Her mind felt free from worry. She couldn't remember the last time she felt uninhibited.

—

Peter watched over Sandra as she prayed that night. He was pleased that she had given Ramla hope, something blessed to cling to. To know that God would be introduced into her life by a wonderful believer uplifted his own soul. Peter contemplated---If only I could remind Sandra that she is a handmaiden for the Lord. Could I ask her to help Ramla get to know God? He gave into his thoughts and reasoned that one instruction would not hurt. Dispersing himself in the moonlight shining through her window, he whispered, "Don't give up on Ramla. She needs you."

Peter then and continued observing Ramla through the Pond of Contemplation.

"Peter, rise from the Pond and appear before God!"

He obeyed the voice and felt himself moving. He saw the burning bush before him, shielded his eyes, and positioned himself on his knees.

"Peter, you have defied my command. You are having thoughts of interfering with my plan for mankind, and your thoughts along with your actions have become sin. What have you to say for yourself? Remember, you have died from the earth and your position is to obey and follow my commands. If your heart cries out for Ramla or anyone else that remains on earth, there is an altar that you can go to and place your petitions before God.

Peter was stunned and wasn't sure what to say in his defense. His soul shook with fear.

"Oh God…I didn't realize I had defied your command. I only wanted to help Ramla come to know you."

"I commanded you to observe Ramla from the Pond of Contemplation. You are not to intervene in her life!"

Peter wracked his mind thinking of what he had done that disobeyed God. He felt a strong, forceful hand upon his head.

"You cannot speak to anyone as an angelic being, your position was explained to you earlier. You must allow the chain of events to happen. My will must be done. By having thoughts about whispering to Sandra and acting upon them, you are defying spiritual laws. It's forbidden!"

Peter understood and was full of remorse for his actions.

"I understand. I didn't know beforehand. What can I do to make amends? I'm so sorry!"

God saw that Peter was sincere and forgave him.

"Peter, the rules of my kingdom must remain intact. Because you intervened, Satan has set a deadline for when Ramla must surrender to me of her own accord. If she doesn't accept by the scheduled date, Armageddon will begin. Be conscious of this. The universe may be forever changed. Now go and observe Ramla."

Peter prayed after God spoke to him. He began to see visions of the earth imploding if Ramla didn't acknowledge and believe that God is real. He knew he had to be careful to only observe. He wanted to do more and knew he had to dispel the desperation he felt inside.

He returned to the Pond of Contemplation. Time had passed in Ramla's life while he was away, Peter had asked to become Ramla's guardian without counting the cost, it was a big responsibility, he still had not learned how to stay focused on the task set before him. She was still living with Mrs. Cox and had given birth to a daughter. She was a beautiful child. "Sammael you are not interested in fatherhood or the day-to-day activities that involved our child."

"Ramla I feel trapped in this relationship, and to be honest with you, I am bored just staying home and helping take care of the baby. Please do not doubt my love for Kareese, she is precious and I enjoy spending daddy time with her, I just feel like you got pregnant in order to escape your mother's house."

" Let me get this straight, did you just say what I thought you said? It takes two to tangle honey."

"Sammael believe what you want, I am going in the kitchen to spend time with your mom."

Mrs. Cox continued frequent conversations over tea with Ramla and always invited her to attend church. Peter knew that he had to be silent and only monitor what was happening. He wanted to do God's will. Patience had been his weakness while on earth. Now he felt the watchful eyes

of the Almighty on him as he worked toward the art of it—
patience.

—

Sandra found Ramla sitting at the kitchen table while
breast-feeding her little one. She loved and admired her
granddaughter but her own son's lack of involvement
saddened her. He should have been a better father to his little
girl.

Like father, like son, she thought.

She was trying her best to speak words of life over her
son but something was getting more and more strange about
him and his actions. Sandra thought back to his earlier years
as a small child. He took delight in destroying things—his
sippy cups, his toys, pretty things around the house. At
twelve she caught him smoking, not cigarettes but
marijuana. Sandra worried for Ramla and felt sad because
she was afraid that the road would be hard and long for her.
Inside she knew that one day, and it probably wouldn't be
long from now, Ramla would have to raise her grandchild
alone, without the help of her son. She looked over at Ramla
this Sunday morning and silently prayed for her and
Kareese, "God, have mercy on them, have mercy."

"How are things going this morning, Ramla?"

"Oh, not too good... I guess. Kareese and I hardly get to see Sammael, but other than that, things are okay." Ramla kept silent on her attempts to visit her own mother and involve her in Kareese's new life. But she wasn't interested. It hurt too much to admit audibly. Even to Mrs. Cox.

Sandra could see the rejection in Ramla's eyes and tried to lift her spirits. She would not tell Ramla that she believed Sammael was seeing another teenage girl that lived not too far from their home. She hated the feelings of indifference and betrayal because she had experienced them herself many times in her past with her husband.

"Do you know what I think we all need?"

"No. What?"

"I think we need to go to church and listen to a powerful sermon and sing for the Lord. Whaddya say?" as she slapped her lap and smiled.

Usually, Ramla politely declined, but this time she felt like she needed to do something that would make her feel better. She was having a hard time dealing with her situation.. She thought for a moment and smiled at Sandra.

"Yes. I would love to go to church with you. Is it alright to bring Kareese?"

"I insist that you bring my darling granddaughter. I want to show her off to my friends. That beautiful smile, those fat legs, and the smell of fresh baby powder will add a little sunshine to the Bible study."

Ramla couldn't believe the gift she was given in Ms. Sandra. Sammael made her life more difficult by not talking to her, he was bitter over the situation and no longer liked Ramla, she was disappointed in her boyfriend but she wouldn't trade anything for her daughter. She couldn't hate Sammael, he had made it possible for her to have her precious child.

That evening, Ramla and Ms. Sandra got ready for church. Together they dressed Kareese in her prettiest outfit. Sandra had a strong feeling that God was going to work a miracle that night, she just knew it. She had been praying and fasting and dreamed that an angel had spoken to her. "Tonight's the night. Praise God!"

six

Sandra and Ramla strolled into the church. Ramla held her baby and was guarded as Sandra hugged each friend and introduced them to her. The ooohs and aaahhhs over her baby brought a sense of pride she hadn't known before. The organ music began to play and Sandra knew it was time for them to take a seat. Instead of taking her regular seat in the middle of the church, Sandra walked to the front and sat down, motioning Ramla to sit next to the aisle.

"Dear, would you mind if I hold Kareese during service?"

"No. Not at all," Ramla said tenderly handing Kareese to her.

Sandra mouthed, "Thank you," and gently began to rock her grandbaby.

Ramla shifted her attention to the pastor. He watched his congregation take their seats and nodded to the choir director. She got lost in the music and kept time by patting her foot. She enjoyed the service and listened intently to the words of the sermon. The pastor talked about the warfare in ones mind, and how Satan's job is to drive people, tempting them to commit all types of sin. He stated that it was up to the people to resist, and once they do, Satan will flee.

---Warfare in my mind, Ramla thought to herself. --- Interesting... I never thought of my worries as warfare.

She felt goose bumps on her arms and her mind begin to ease. She watched as gold collection plates were passed down each aisle and didn't respond to them until Sandra leaned over and explained that Jesus taught his followers they should give tithes and offerings to the church. Ramla witnessed it first hand when Sandra paid tithes for both of them. Sandra had seen the power of tithing and knew for a fact that it would be a blessing to all who participated.

Once, when she was in church praying, she closed her eyes and began to worship God, imagining she was in heaven dancing at the throne. She loved it when her mind's eye was free to travel there. In her daydream, she saw something awesome. She saw herself kneel down and put her two hands together, extending them in front of her as if to receive something from a man that was walking towards her. The man who looked like Jesus full of glory began pouring seeds into her hands. She believed the gesture meant that he was supplying all of her needs. Then she saw angels bringing the tithes and prayer requests before him. A window had opened and another angel began pouring out seeds all over the land, blessing the people of God who had been faithful with their giving. By faith, gifts were being activated all over the land; the minds of people opened up and they began writing down inventions, goals and plans that would prosper them. It was amazing. Her life would never be the same after this experience.

She thought of another time she was in church and began to think about insurance. She thought it was a strange idea because she had little money and felt it was a waste of resources to bid on death, at such a young age. *"Well, I am not going to figure this one out on my own, but will pray about it and allow God to lead me."* To Sandra's surprise, Brother Barry Tucker and his wife walked by.

"Hello Brother and Sister Tucker. My best friend Denise told me that you two sell insurance. I'm interested in a policy. Can we meet?"

"Sister Sandra, it is a good thing to think ahead. One never knows what might happen in the future. Please give us a call and we will be happy to assist you."

From that point on Sandra became emotional when she placed her money in the plate. She knew without a doubt God was working on her behalf.

Just then, an elder said to the congregation the exact thing Sandra had witnessed in her mind. She sat in her seat amazed at the confirmation that was coming forth through the mouth of the elder.

"The Almighty opened a huge window and began pouring blessings in the form of wisdom upon his people, the type that brings about prosperity when activated from within to those that believe. For it is in his wisdom and all-knowing power that God will lead the pastors after his own heart on how to govern the tithe. Our pastor has shown steadfastness and good stewardship over the money that has come into this ministry. Can I get an Amen? The last thing God wants to see is pastors gambling at a casino with the tithe, or robbing the people of God. When we handle God's business, he handles our business, and takes good care of his own. We must honor God with our tithes!"

"Hallelujah! Thank you, Jesus!" Sandra shouted.

The pastor stood up and held his hand out for the elder to pass him the microphone. He called for people to join him up front. Warm tears flowed from Ramla's eyes and she felt compelled to go up to the altar. She turned to Sandra then assumed that is why Sandra asked to hold Kareese and offered her the aisle seat. Ramla stood up and walked to the front, unaware of what was going to happen or why she needed to be there.

Instinctively, Ramla kneeled before the pastor as others joined her. She bowed her head and began to cry. She was remorseful over all the sins she committed and troubled by the trauma she endured. She felt her load lighten as she prayed, and cried until her dress was soaked with tears.

"Hallelujah! Brothers and sisters! Sister Sandra has brought to us a child of God!" the pastor exclaimed.

He knelt in front of Ramla, placed his hand on her head and prayed.

"Dear God, this young lady is kneeling before you and needs to know your love. I pray that she will come to know and love Jesus, our Lord. Develop a relationship with him and walk a path that will lead to her destiny in Jesus name amen.

God and Jesus are love and they have been waiting for this moment. He will heal your hurts and mend your broken heart. However, it is up to you to stir up the gifts that are inside of you. Can I get an amen?" he shouted.

Ramla trembled and wept. She could feel love and hope filling her soul. She wanted to be a good Christian. She wanted to believe what the pastor preached was true. All she knew was that his words surpassed her limited thinking, her doubts, and most importantly to her, the fears that had haunted her most of her life. Chill bumps ran up her arms as she tried to embrace the feelings of peace she was experiencing. The guilt and shame departed from her.

"Can you feel God's presence brothers and sisters? He's showing his love, it is overflowing. Another soul has been rescued from the hands of the devil. Praise him! Hallelujah!" The church exploded as the people shouted amen and hallelujah.

After the service was over, the entire congregation took turns hugging and praying for Ramla. They knew they watched something special but didn't comprehend the depths of God's power to yet be revealed through her life.

When it was time to leave, Sandra drove and sang hymns all the way back home. Ramla was still moved to tears by the experience and Kareese sat quietly in her car seat, her eyes heavy and drifting back off to sleep.

"Child, praise be unto Jesus! I could tell there was a reason you were sent to me. I was supposed to bring you to the church."

When they got home, Ramla put her daughter to bed. She and Sandra talked almost half the night about what they had experienced at church. Ramla felt whole and safe in God's love. She stayed even after Sandra went to sleep, praying and thanking Jesus for showing her the way.

—

Peter witnessed the event then shouted and ran around the Pool of Contemplation.

"Praise God! She made it, her test is complete!" he bellowed.

An angel saw the universe opened to Ramla but Ramala was unaware of the provisions set before her in the spirit realm. They would not be released until she decided to claim the victory for life and speak the words of God to undo the curses that had been placed over her by the enemy.

Ramla heard and acted on what was preached. The pastor told them the importance of reading the Bible, praying and being obedient to the things learned. Ramla couldn't put her Bible down, it was special to her because Mrs. Cox gave it to her for her Christmas. For the first time in her life, her soul was thirsty and she was able to understand what the Bible was conveying, most of it still a mystery to her young mind, however she longed for truth and held it close for many days.

—

Jesus appeared to Peter and clarified what was yet to be done.

"Peter, Ramla has been introduced to God. She will now endure trials and rely on his wisdom and strength to get her through. The timeline is still in effect."

"Oh, Lord! How much time does she have? If she falls short, when will Armageddon begin?"

"Sooner than you think, Peter. She will have ample time to come to the throne and honor the kingdom of God with her faith and obedience. Keep watching, and remember your vow to My Father."

Jesus was concerned because he knew that Ramla wouldn't embrace her new faith in the beginning. Her mind had to be renewed with the bread of life and it would take intense intercession from others on her behalf in order to overcome her past.

Peter knew that he was not to question Jesus any further about the timeline. The clock was ticking and Ramla's trials would either end the world or save it.

She had no idea how much depended on her obedience to God's will. She was a key player in his kingdom. If she fully understood the power she possessed and the importance of her existence, she would sacrifice whatever the spirit of God requested, especially a sick relationship, one that will only harm her in the future, and be able to heal from the devastation of her past.

Jesus pleaded with his Father to have mercy on her because she had not yet developed a mind to fully obey his ways. He also knew that Satan would turn up the heat and Ramla would have to endure to the end.

Jesus uttered one more word to Peter, "Faith."

The angels in heaven worshipped God, and rejoiced because Ramla had surrendered her heart to Jesus. At that moment, Jesus began to weep and intercede for her. He knew that this was just the beginning and she still had much to learn. He summoned one of the angels to immediately wrap his wings around her to convince her of the Father's love.

"Angel of Destiny, show an act of kindness to Ramla and make sure she doesn't loose heart."

—

Ramla began to cry and a sensation of overwhelming love flowed around her body bringing about a self-confidence she had not known in the pass. She didn't understand why, but she reasoned that it was a sign of God's unconditional love for her. This was the first time she realized she had a friend Jesus. He loved her and remembered when her spirit was first transported from heaven to earth. Jesus felt the price paid for Ramla's soul more than anyone. Ramla was one of the souls for whom he shed his blood on Calvary. He trembled at the thought of her surrendering her soul to Satan any longer through ingnorance.

Later that night, Sammael came home, tip-toeing through the front door, he was coming from his new girlfriends house around the corner, trying to be quiet so he wouldn't wake Ramla and Kareese. He knew his mother was asleep as well and decided he would simply look in on Ramla, and then go to his own bedroom. He quietly padded across the wooden floor and sat on the side of her bed. He watched for awhile and noticed that she was sleeping peacefully. The moonlight spilled over her face and he bent down to kiss her.

The boy in Sammael wanted her, but the evolving man decided to let her sleep. It was as if he felt someone goading him to take advantage of her. Was it the innocence he had to have or the conquest? He didn't know. His flesh was selfish, two women in one night was exciting to him. He decided to leave before he did something he would later regret. Just as he was getting on his feet, Ramla stirred and groggily asked him what he was doing.

"Just watching you. Go back to sleep."

"Sammael…."

"What is it?"

Ramla sat up and gave him a soft kiss. She felt married in every sense of the word. Sammael returned the kiss and became aware that he was losing control, so he backed away. He was walking away from a sure thing; something had a hold on him. Sammael felt confused by his own actions and Ramla noticed. She looked in his eyes and saw the smoldering heat. It was the flesh that he denied.

Ramla had to admit that she admired Sammael's body and handsome face more than ever; however the words of the pastor came to her mind, "God will make a way of escape for you." She wondered why she remembered that statement and thought it was strange. Ramla knew what the words meant and turned from the desires of her flesh. She took a deep breath and yielded for the first time to the Spirit of God. She longed to tell Sammael about church, but knew he wouldn't be interested.

That morning, Sammael smiled at her as she walked into the kitchen to feed Kareese. A note was posted on the refrigerator from Sandra. "Got in very late from work last night. Exhausted. Will sleep in. Love, Mom/Sandra."

Ramla grinned at the note. It was just like her to be so thoughtful. She forgot that Sandra had to go to work after church last night. She was more indebted to Sandra than she would ever know.

Ramla began to fix breakfast for Sammael and Kareese, the formula was warming in the pot, bacon and eggs sent an aroma through the house, humming a hymn she remembered from the night before Ramla was confident that Ms. Cox had taught her all she needed to know about cooking. The song felt good to her soul.

"Hey, when Mom wakes up, you want to take a walk?" Sammael eyed Ramla anxiously for her answer.

"Sure, I guess that would be okay. That way, she can watch Kareese."

"Yeah! I was thinking that too."

Sandra walked down the hall, uncharacteristically sluggish in her bathrobe and slippers. She greeted them and sat at the kitchen table as Ramla poured her a fresh cup of tea..

"Sammael, pass the sugar, reach in the fridge and hand me some cream."

"Good morning, Mrs. Cox. How did you sleep?"

"Oh, child, I slept like a baby once I got into my bed. I didn't get home until three o'clock. The supervisor let me work a little late and gave me tonight off. It'll be early to bed tonight, that's for sure."

"Say Mom, Ramla and I are going to go for a walk. Will you watch Kareese?"

"Sure, I never miss a chance to baby-sit my beautiful granddaughter!"

The three of them ate breakfast together, just like a real family. Ramla longed for a gold band to wear on her finger. She wondered if it was a good sign that he wanted to take a walk today, just the two of them. Ramla gathered the dirty dishes and began cleaning the kitchen when Sandra told her and Sammael to skedaddle. She would take care of Kareese and clean up later. Ramla thanked her and Sammael opened the door for her as they left the house.

Sammael and Ramla sauntered down the sidewalk for awhile without saying anything. Ramla was dying of curiosity as to why he wanted to leave the house with her. She glanced at him and admired his beautiful chocolate skin. He had a swagger and a confidence about him that was undeniable. That's why so many girls found him attractive. "Sammael? Where are we going?"

"Oh, to a place downtown. There's a movie I want you to see with me." My friends father owes a video store and he allows us to visit the store during early morning hours.

Ramla beamed. She was excited that Sammael was taking her to a movie. She hoped that their dating would lead to marriage, so they could be a legitimate family. They walked for awhile longer and made it to downtown. She held onto Sammael's arm as they passed drunkards, prostitutes and homeless people. Sammael finally stopped and pulled some money out of his pocket to pay admission. Ramla looked up at the marquee and saw naked women and the letters XXX beside them.

"Sammael? We're not going in there, are we?"

"It's okay, baby…you'll love it. I promise."

He was growing increasingly frustrated with his own behavior, his conscience was bothering him. He had something nasty planned for the two of them. He wanted to act out his fantasias and react to Ramla as he normally did with the other women he snuck around with. In his heart he knew Ramla would not agree, still he decided to try her anyway.

Sammael purchased their tickets and led her inside the dark theater where a few men were already seated watching the film. Ramla was repulsed and reminded of her summer with Alice. She couldn't believe her eyes. She saw women with women, three men with one woman, a group of women with one man, all performing acts she had never imagined. Sammael watcher her as she tried to keep her eyes ahead on the screen. When he stopped watching her, she closed her eyes. He was excited by the porn movie. She bit her nails counting the minutes until it would be over. She knew this wasn't good for her. The feeling of sadness that had left her the night she was in church was returning and she felt shame and guilt.

The movie was finally over and the lights remained low. Ramla looked around and saw what she was sure were hookers and thought that she was probably the only woman that wasn't. She couldn't understand why Sammael was was interested in porn; she wondered if he had a serious problem that she didn't know about. He seemed obsessed with it.

"Did you like it?"

"Uh….it was different."

"Come here with me."

Sammael led her out of the theatre and next door to a rundown hotel. He paid the dirty looking clerk for a room. The rumpled twenty would buy them an hour.

"Room twelve, last one on the left," he directed.

Sammael took the key, and noticed a hooker standing in back of them, looking him up and down.

"Hey baby, ya wanna have a good time?"

Sammael stared back and smirked.

"How much?"

"Twenty-five bucks for thirty minutes."

Sammael fished deep into his pockets and gave her the bills.

"Come on....I want you to show my girlfriend how it's done."

Ramla stood there, feeling much like a hooker herself. She was sick to her stomach and afraid to speak up for herself. Sammael showed the hooker to their room and opened the door for them. The room was tiny with a scruffy bed and an open door that revealed a commode. Sammael turned to Ramla and was serious for a moment. Dread came over her; fearing him when he acted that way. Her mind traveled back to the time when Sammael slapped her by surprise the last time he had that look in his eyes. This time she couldn't tell if he wanted to hit her or just have raunchy sex.

"Ramla, I want you to watch us so you can do this later for me. "What's your name, sugar?"

"Roxie", she replied. "Time is ticking away honey, you wanna do it or not?"

Sammael reached over to kiss Roxie and was surprised when she turned away.

"I never kiss clients. You can have the rest of me though."

"Fine by me."

Sammael stripped off his clothes and Roxie took off her short skirt and tight blouse. She knelt in front of Sammael and took him in her mouth. Ramla watched, horrified to witness such a personal and intimate act. She could tell Sammael was enjoying it as Roxie expertly maneuvered him. He briefly turned to make sure Ramla was watching. Roxie knew exactly how to please this man she had never met before and didn't know anything about. It was strictly physical. Ramla noticed that she appeared to be an actress, totally uninvolved with him personally, yet knowing when to make noises, move a certain way, slow down or speed up. She guessed it was from many years of practice just like this. Ramla saw that Sammael was oblivious to Roxie herself. All he knew was that he was having multiple and wild sensations and was trying to experience them all.

Ramla's fear subsided and she began to enjoy watching Sammael's arousal, but was jealous and sickened by Roxie at the same time. When Roxie knew that Sammael was ready to ejaculate, she moved back from him, looked at her watch and brought things to an abrupt halt.

"What are you doing?" Sammael screamed.

"You owe me another twenty-five, honey. Thirty minutes has gone by and I have to make a living."

Sammael could hardly move and Ramla knew he was worked up in a bad way. He began cursing and yelling for Ramla to hand him his wallet. She reached over and got it out of his trousers and handed it to him. He gave her the twenty-five, but Roxie refused. She told him she was bored and sick of him. He slapped her so hard that she fell across the bed and didn't move. Sammael grabbed his clothes and quickly put them on. He reached for Ramla's hand, and they ran down the hallway and out the front door of the hotel towards a bus. He flagged down the driver. They climbed aboard, huffing and puffing, exhausted from their quick getaway.

Sammael leaned his head back on the seat and looked over at Ramla. "Why are you looking so crazy? I hoped you learned something from Roxie. That's the kind of woman that can take care of me."

Ramla couldn't believe that she had just been taken to an X-rated movie and a sleazy hotel where she was to watch a hooker perform sex on what she considered her man. She had enjoyed it for a moment, yes, but now felt confused, resentful, and sad.

One thing for sure, she knew that this event, too, had changed her. No sixteen year-old should have to witness such things. She knew she had lost respect for Sammael and felt her desire for him slipping away.

"Come on, we get off of the bus at the next stop."

Ramla and Sammael walked the rest of the way home. After about ten minutes in silence, Sammael gathered the courage to speak.

"So, did you like it?" being careful to not look her directly in the face.

"No."

"Why?"

"Because you are *my* man and I didn't like some hooker having her way with you. What's wrong with you?" Ramla bit her lip trying to hold back the tears.

Sammael put his hands deep into his jean pockets and sighed. "Look, Ramla. I'm sorry. I wanted this to be a nice surprise for you. It's that we never get time alone, just us. We're constantly worrying if Mom is coming home early from work," his voice trailed off. "Look, I really like you, a lot. All I'm saying is that if you won't... then I'll have to get another girlfriend. Do you understand what I'm saying?"

Ramla started to panic. She thought she loved Sammael, and wanted their family to stay together. She still had warp ideas about sex. She apologized so that she could keep her man, but on the inside her resentment deepened.

"I'm sorry, Sammael....forgive me?"

Ramla looked at him in the eye and sensed that he forgave her. She felt a bit of relief and dread at the same time. She knew she had to try and hold on for the sake of their child. Sammael really did not help with his daughter, however Ramla felt Kareese needed both parents. She contemplated,   ---I just need to have more patience with Sammael. Maybe soon he will mature into a man who is not so selfish, one who will really love us and think about things other than where to stick his penis.

—

"Well, well, well......it took some doing angels, but I do think I've created a sex monster. What do you think?" Satan mocked. "Since I know you were watching, Peter, allow me to explain."

"I know what happened. No explanation necessary," said Peter. He was exasperated by what he just witnessed.

"No Peter, there is more to this," replied the angel of destiny.

"Thank you. Now, as I was saying...I have manifested my power into every soul that was in that theater—the whores, deviates, perverts, Sammael, and even Ramla. If you were watching, the lights never went up. This is one place in which the light will not totally overcome the darkness. It's my darkness, my pure evil that flourishes there. You could hear the demons moan, see the lusting souls congregate, almost taste for yourself their vile and wicked hunger. I burned an unquenchable desire to engage in illicit sex into every soul there. They were all infected with my poison. There is no sanctity in marriage. Cheating on spouses or innocent partners is encouraged, especially if a sexual disease can be passed on." Satan rasped. "Peter, surely you know my evilness runs deep in Roxie and Sammael. By being in the same room, Ramla has been tainted as well. Oh, and Roxie has delivered my most potent sexual vice. She was able to directly inflame Sammael's soul with such a lust, that he is unable to escape the madness of my licentious power. The prostitute was used to set fire set fire in his lions! He couldn't move!" Satan roared in triumph.

"So what was in it for Roxie?" Peter asked, seething with anger.

"Fifty-bucks, I reward my messengers well, don't I?"

Peter filled with anger, but knew he couldn't interfere with Ramla's fate. He watched with sadness as lust took over Sammael. The other angels had watched too and knew what Satan said was true.

Satan pondered for awhile, "Gee, angels....I was thinking. What if Sammael were to use Ramla and then dump her? Where would she go next?" Satan chuckled.

"Ramla still has Mrs. Cox," said the angel of destiny. "Ramla will reach her destiny with her help."

"Hmmm...afraid not. Since Peter, your weak little angel of faith, dabbled in her life, I'm taking Mrs. Cox out of the equation. She secretly has a root of bitterness that is eating her alive. Shame on you, Peter! Now, Ramla will never fulfill her destiny because of you."

Peter was stunned and stared into the Pond of Contemplation heavy with regret. He had already begged God to forgive him for his past interference. Again he wanted to do something, but knew he had to simply observe.

"Peter, don't involve others in her life. You are to only monitor!" scolded the angel of destiny.

"I shall, Destiny. I shall."

He was going to play strictly by the plan that God set for Ramla.

—

When Ramla and Sammael returned home, Mrs. Cox was sitting at the kitchen table holding Kareese and crying. Ramla was alarmed and sat beside her.

"What's wrong?"

"I have learned that my mother and aunt have both fallen gravely ill. Sammael and I are the only family they have and we must go home to North Carolina to attend to them. I'm afraid with finances as they are, I'll need Sammael there to work full-time while I tend to their care. I'm so sorry, but there won't be enough room or money to take you and Karesse with us," she sobbed.

Satan looked on and laughed because he knew that the events where taking place just as he had planned. Evil was all around. Mrs. Cox was confused and not thinking clearly surely she could have found a way to take care of her granddaughter.

Ramla was incredulous. She couldn't believe her world was about to be turned upside down again. She felt bad for Mrs. Cox, but began to panic. She didn't know how she would care for herself and the baby.

"Don't worry, Ms. Sandra, Kareese and I will be fine. I promise."

"Child, I know you don't want to live with your mother, and I know you can't live with your father. Where do you want to go? I need to know that you will be taken care of."

Ramla thought for a moment and decided that she would like to live in Washington, D.C.

"Why in the District? Do you have family there?"

Mrs. Cox sounded hopeful, and Ramla didn't want her to worry, so she lied and told her that she had a cousin that lived near the Capitol. In actuality, she wanted to start over, and getting out of town was the best way to do it. She was numb. It would just be the two of them.

"I'll pack my things."

"I'll buy you a bus ticket, dear. I'm so sorry about all of this."

Ramla walked to her room and began putting their things into her suitcase. Mrs. Cox had already left an envelope containing $200 on her bed. It was all the money she had.

Samuel kissed Ramla and Kareese goodbye. With a smirk on his face, he made Ramla promise to write when she got to the city. He made a vow to take care of Kareese once he got a job. "I will send you money every month to buy diapers, milk and clothes for Kareese. Just be careful."

" Wow, finally that burden is lifted from my shoulders, I thought I would have to deal with raising a child for years to come, Sammael thought to himself."

Ramla hugged Sammael, and her heart felt like it was crumbling into tiny pieces. She was being separated from the man she loved, a woman she had adopted as mother, and the most secure home she had known .

Ramla asked Mrs. Cox to watch Karese for her while she ran to tell her mother what was happening.

While knocking on the door, Ramla noticed a foreclosure sign on the door. No one was home.

An hour later, Ramla and Kareese were at the bus stop with a one-way ticket to Washington D. C. Ramla alone would have to fend for them. She boarded the bus with Kareese in her carrier and took a seat. The bus pulled out of the terminal and began making its way north. She rested her head on the cool window and watched the buildings pass by.

"Why, God? Why? Why are you allowing this to happen to me? I'm tired. I wish that I was never born. My life is crazy. I must have been a mistake. If it wasn't for Karesse I would commit suicide. That's right, kill myself. I'm too young for all of this. God if you are real, help us. Please, we need your help. I have made many mistakes in my life. Forgive me and protect us," Ramla pleaded.

Kareese started to cry. It was as if she sensed something was wrong with her mother. Ramla rocked her back and forth, trying to quiet her down for the journey ahead.

seven

After fifteen hours and as many stops, the bus pulled into the Greyhound station in Washington, D.C. Ramla clumsily stood up and waited her turn to exit the bus. Kareese was asleep. She made her way to the nearest phone booth and opened the directory. She needed to find somewhere to stay that was cheap and safe. She would begin to look for a job in the morning, she had no other choice but to take Kareese with her..

"Hello, Super Eight? I'm at the bus depot. Do you have a clerk that can come and get me? I need a room tonight for my daughter and me."

"Who do you think you are, the Queen? Get your own flippin' way down here," the desk clerk grunted.

Ramla was startled by this reaction and began to cry.

—

Peter watched Ramla. He had an idea. He asked the angel of destiny to lightly place his forefinger in the pond on the face of an older woman waiting in line for the phone. She needed financial assistance because she was a widow and didn't have enough money to fill her prescriptions. Peter began to see much more clearly. He smiled, as he knew that God approved of his action.

"Thank you, God," Peter prayed.

"What are you doing boy?" Satan shouted.

"Did you interfere with Ramla's life again?"

"No, Satan. I'm simply asking the angel of destiny to allow a woman to experience wisdom regarding her finances. Ramla doesn't know her, and she will not ask anything of her. This woman will go her own way, never to see Ramla again. The world can't stop because Ramla is being tested. Is that fair?"

Satan was silent for a split second. "You are not interfering at all in Ramla's life? None of these people will interact with her?"

"Absolutely not."

"Continue."

And Peter smiled.

—

Ramla decided to take a cab and stepped out into the street to hail one. Out of nowhere, a car squealed its tires as it sped around the corner, headed directly for her. She was frozen with fear and couldn't move; believing she was going to die. Michael the arch angel appeared and stood in front of Ramla and turned the car. It hit a lamp pole instead. Michael guided Ramla and her baby to a safe place, and directed a cab to stop for them. Peter was amazed at the angel's ability to stop the accident.

Just then, Peter remembered almost losing his life while driving down Main Street. The same occurred with Ramla as it did with him. A car that was recklessly headed towards him seemed to have been thrown into the opposite direction too. For the first time he understood what had actually happened on that cold winter morning. But, he thought, if Michael could stop the car from killing Ramla, why didn't he stop her father from raping her?

"Peter your thoughts are many," Michael responded. "The heart of man is deceitfully wicked. Ramla's father listened to the voice of the evil one, refusing to obey the voice of God's spirit. Some things you will never understand. Our job is to obey God's leading, and follow his instructions. To step in and stop Davis would have meant that I would defy the laws of the spiritual and natural realms. Davis is a human with free will. The car I just stopped is a material object. That didn't show my interference."

Peter shook his head, not understanding what he had just heard, but in his heart, he was willing to accept the fact that all things work together for the good of those that love Christ Jesus.

Satan was furious and shouted at the arch angel, "You can't intervene in Ramla's life by saving her!"

"And you can't purposely kill her either. The angels will save her every time you try. Be warned," Michael threatened.

"Holy Spirit, touch the cab driver's heart so that he will help Ramla," the arch angel petitioned as he disappeared into the heavens.

—

"Sir, can you tell me where the nearest motel is located? I'm short on money, and my daughter and I need a place to stay that is safe."

The pleading look in Ramla's eyes won over the cabbie.

"Get in. It's on the house."

A man already sat in the back seat and did not speak to Ramla, he only repeated his destination to the cabbie. The cabbie informed Ramla that he would drop the gentlemen off first and then get her a motel room. Ramla looked up and noticed the cab driver's license information. She decided to make a mental note of his ID number, just in case she experienced something out of the ordinary. He drove up to the fancy hotel, and the man in the back got out and tipped him.

"Thank ya, sir. Now let's get you to the motel."

He saw a nice-looking motel and pulled in.

"C'mon, this place is very reasonable and safe. Rod will take care of ya. He's sitting at the front desk."

They walked into the lobby and the cabbie rang the bell.

"Hey Mr. Rod, my man. How's it goin'?"

The cabbie and Rod pumped hands in a friendly shake.

"Not too bad, Ira. And who do we have here?"

Rod eyed Ramla suspiciously and saw that she had a baby with her. Kareese was nestled in her carrier without a care.

"She's short on money, man, and needs a room for awhile so she can get on her feet."

Rod winked at Ira and asked Ramla to sign the register.

"How much does it cost a night, sir?" Ramla anxiously asked.

"Fifteen bucks a night, kiddo."

She signed the register and fished for the money that Mrs. Cox had given her.

'Oh, you don't pay until you leave. That's the way it always works."

"Joe, grab her bag and show her to Room 17."

Ramla thanked the two gentlemen and walked with Joe the bellman to her room.

"Say, man....you know, she's underage. And, with a baby too," Rod shook his head.

"I know, but she looked so lost. Look dude, I'm paying for her first week here. I'll be back in about an hour to bring her and the baby some food."

He laid out the money he had earned since early in the morning. He then drove to a grocery store and bought a loaf of bread, baby food, sandwich meat and several bottles of soda, juice and milk. He also stopped and got her a crab cake sandwich and fries for dinner. He raced into the motel and loaded Rod down with the supplies and waved goodbye.

Joe turned the key into Ramla's room and opened the door for her. She had not stayed in a motel before. There was a small refrigerator, a large bed, dresser, end table, television set and bathroom. She was awestruck. Joe turned on the television for her and handed her the remote. He also explained how the air conditioner worked in the room. She thanked him. When he casually held his hand out for a tip, she shook it. He shrugged and closed the door behind him.

Ramla sat on the bed and looked at the hotel guide. She wondered what she would eat that night, if anything. She at least had to make sure Kareese was fed.

Suddenly, there was a knock at the door. With caution, she opened it. Rod stood there with a grocery sack full of items. He chastised her for not first looking through the peephole.

"Miss Ramla, Ira, the cabbie brought this to you. He said it was from the Welcome to D.C. Committee."

He handed her the bag, closed the door behind him and shouted to her from the other side of the door, "Lock the door behind me, Miss Ramla!"

"Yes sir!"

Ramla chained and locked the door. She combed through the bag; it smelled delicious. The milk, juice, soda and lunchmeat were refrigerated and she put the bread on the dresser. She found the crab cake sandwich, fries, and baby food. She fed Kareese first, then burped, changed and laid her on the bed beside her. She watched television and gorged her meal. She was so grateful; she hardly knew how to react. She crawled under the covers and grabbed the remote. With her toes curled and cozy and her knees pulled together, she flipped the channels just for the fun of it. A little while later the phone rang.

"Miss Ramla, I forgot to tell ya. Ira paid for you to stay here a week."

"I don't know how to thank him."

"I do. Make something of yourself, take good care of that baby, and do something nice for a stranger. Good night, Miss Ramla."

Ramla put her head into her hands and cried.

—

Later that week, Ira came to visit her and turned her on to the idea of working as a receptionist for a cab company until she was an experienced driver. She'd have a lot to do beginning with learning to drive. But he was willing to help her and vouch for her age. He knew she was responsible for her daughter and didn't question her about it. He was the first fatherly figure that didn't try to abuse her in anyway. She felt comfortable around him.

The money she made helped to pay the bills, and she was able to take Kareese with her. It was a dangerous job, offered no health insurance, but it was a living. After being a receptionist and driving a cab for many years, she was getting tired of it. She routinely read the classifieds to find a better job. On nights when the fares were slow and the only life in the city seemed to be nightlights that twinkled and music that blared, her thoughts floated back to when she first came to the District at seventeen with a baby in tow.

She sighed and saw three women trying to flag her down. They looked like they had had one too many, and were too young to be out this late. Ramla steered her cab over to the corner and picked them up.

"Where to?"

"The Wyndham," one of the girls giggled.

"Which one?"

Ramla could tell she was going to get tired of these girls quick.

"Baltimore!"

Ramla turned around to make sure she heard right. Not that Baltimore was that far away, but it was a bit of a distance, and it would take some time to get back. At least the fare would be substantial. She was exhausted but she drove for awhile and chit-chatted with them.

"Are you girls from out of town?"

Ramla glanced in her rearview mirror admiring the leather jacket one of them wore. Waiting for their answer, she yawned, and reminded herself to keep her eyes on the road. They were busy chattering away. Ramla asked them again above the laughter, "Are you girls from out of town?"

She knew full well that they were. They had all the markings of strangers.

"Yes ma'am," they snickered.

Judging from their accents, Ramla knew they must be from the south; northerners don't talk like that. She decided to swing by the White House to give the girls a quick look. They were paying for it. At once, all three girls gasped.

"Oh my God! There are so many homeless people sitting outside of the White House. Fran, look at them. Look at that woman. She looks crazy!"

"Which one?"

"That one. The woman with the hair standing on end."

The girls pointed and giggled.

Ramla was accustomed to the city and its inhabitants. She had only slowed the cab so the girls could get a better look at the Capitol. But then she saw the woman they were talking about. Her hair and her eyes looked wild. Slowing way down, Ramla looked closer to make out the woman's features and was ceased by panic. It was her mother.

She had stopped by her mother's house several years ago to let her know she was moving to Washington, D.C. and to show Eva her granddaughter, but hadn't laid eyes on her since she left town. Ramla suddenly felt twelve again and was watching her mother talking to people that weren't there. The sight of her was like a knife driven through her chest. She wanted to stop, wanted to cry, but couldn't because she didn't want the girls to know. Their laughter directed at her mother drove the knife deeper.

Ramla accelerated, fighting back tears and regaining her control, hoping that somehow her mother would still be there when she would return hours later. One of the songs she had learned years ago in church came to her mind and she drove on and began humming the words to encourage herself. Ramla tried to keep her mind centered on God, but there was a vice gripping her.

Seeing her mother in that condition was heartbreaking. She looked destitute and in poor health, burned from the sun that she most likely lingered in all day long.

Ramla drove on to Baltimore not saying anything further to her passengers until they arrived at their destination.

"Girls, that'll be $137.50."

"Yes ma'am, here ya go. One hundred and fifty dollars, keep the change."

"Thank you."

And the giggly girls climbed out of her cab and walked into the Wyndham as if they owned it. Ramla turned her cab around so fast that her tires screeched. She was headed back to the White House with her foot heavy on the gas.

The night felt sobering to Ramla. She hoped and prayed that her mother was still there so she could get her to return home with her. It seemed like an uncommonly long trip. Ramla's pulse was rapid, and her hands were tightly gripped around the stirring wheel, as if holding it with intensity would make the car go faster. She blew her horn at the driver in front of her, upset because she was moving too slow. Then she noticed the handicap license plate. "Oops! I am sorry. Maybe you are God's way of slowing me down."

She finally arrived in the glow of the White House. In the distance she could barely make out the sharp-shooters on top. She noticed that the street that led to the front of the White House was blocked off with barriers, so she made a U-turn, drove a half block down then made a left turn on the next street. She activated the emergency flashers and stepped out of the car. She noticed that her mother had moved to the side where cars were allowed to park. Ramla jumped back in the car and pulled into a parking space. With trepidation, she walked up to her mother.

"Momma, is that you?"

The old woman turned around and glared at her with unknowing eyes. They bulged and offered no hint of recognition. Ramla reached out without thinking to pat her mother's hair down.

"Child, I'm not your momma. I'm King David!"

The old woman stood up and began dancing around Ramla, praising Jehovah's name.

"Mother, please be quiet and calm down. I'm Ramla. Don't you recognize me? I'm your daughter. You're not King David. Can you understand me?"

Ramla's eyes filled with tears as she tried to tell the old woman who she was. "Your name is Eva. Momma, don't you remember?"

"Praise me, child. Praise your Lord. I'm standing before you. I hear your prayers every night."

"Momma, please....come with me to my apartment. You look so thin and tired. Have you eaten?" Ramla pleaded with her mother, but she flatly refused. "If I get you something, will you at least eat it?" Ramla saw that she was getting no where fast with her, so she decided to make a quick trip to McDonalds anyway. She came back and talked with her for awhile. "Here ya go, Momma. Do you remember your granddaughter? Kareese...please try to remember."

Ramla tore off small pieces of a hamburger and put it in Eva's mouth. She slowly chewed it and stared blankly ahead looking neither at the food or her daughter. Ramla fed her more and let her sip coffee. She must have been hungry because she ate every bit of the burger and fries. It was unlike her, she had been a light eater at best. Aunt Mae always said Momma was so thin because she ate like a bird.

"Momma, what in the world brought you to Washington, D.C.? Was it me? What was it?"

Eva remained catatonic until Ramla had asked the last question. She raised her hand and held it over Ramla's forehead.

"Mark my words, girl. You shall see me again. All of heaven is watching you. This world rests on your shoulders. Ramla, you are destined for great things....don't let him win!" Eva thrust her clenched fist in the air and shouted, "Don't let him win. Don't let him win. Don't' let him win."

"Momma, who? Don't let who win?"

Eva's eyes were wide and excited with the spirit. Her hair blew wistfully in the early morning air. Ramla gazed at her mother as she prophesied over her. The street lamps were shining on her mother as the night gave way to morning. The look in her eyes said she was overhearing a conversation.

Ramla sat kneeled on her heel before her mother. She knew her mother was insane, but at the same time speaking truth. It was someone's truth. She just didn't know if she was to accept it as her truth, but it sure felt like it.

Ramla had to ask her again, "Momma, who are you talking about? Who shouldn't win?"

"Satan!" her mother hissed.

Ramla was struck by the message and shivered. As much as she wanted to take her mother home, she knew it was a lost cause. So, she left her in front of the White House, staring at the gate as if waiting for it to magically open. When her mother behaved that way, she couldn't handle her. Her mother needed to see a doctor. Ramla would see to it.

Ramla drove up to her apartment building and turned her lights off. The sun was just about to rise and Kareese would soon be waking up for school. The night sitter had to go home, and she requested Ramla pay her for staying to the wee hours of the morning. Ramla reached in her wallet and paid the woman what she asked for.

Ramla couldn't seem to shake the image of her mother prophesying over her. "Mark my words, girl. You shall see me again. All of heaven is watching you. This world rests upon your shoulders, Ramla. You are destined for great things." It ran through her mind over and over again.

She walked into Kareese's room and found her standing up next to her bed and smiling. She had heard her mother's voice and was waiting for her to come get her. Kareese started bouncing up and down, reaching out to her young mother. Ramla sat on the bed next to her and gently placed her on her lap.

"Baby, it's time to go to school. Come on, Momma will make you breakfast."

She yawned and jumped off of her mother's lap. Kareese started her day as usual, believing that everything was the same—normal.

Ramla couldn't shake it. Something was different. It was in the air. The word "destiny" resonated so profoundly that she began to wonder about her fate. Seeing her mother was not an accident, it was as if she was led to drive to the White House. She wondered if her mother really was speaking some Truth that she needed to take seriously. Her life was important and there was a greater plan for her future. She knew it sure wasn't being a cabbie, although she would always be grateful to Ira for getting her started in the business.

Ramla saw her daughter off to school. She tried to get a little rest before her next shift, but was too deep in thought.

"Destiny" kept ringing through her ears, but she didn't know how or what to do about it. She was getting frustrated. She saw a glimmer of what goodness in life was through Sandra Cox, however, she just couldn't envision it for herself. She drifted and eventually fell asleep.

Several hours later Ramla woke up, made a cup of coffee and read the headlines from the newspaper. She saw a classified ad for a local plant. The company was hiring workers. She read with interest the type of skills needed for the available positions. She had taken a typing class in school, and decided that she could at least try for a clerk's job. She circled the information with a red pen and put it with her purse. She dressed a little nicer than usual, and dropped by the hiring office before her shift started. Ramla had an inkling that this was meant to be. All she had done since she arrived in the District was to drive a cab. She was tiring of the hours and the strangers that she picked up daily. Once she had gotten robbed, and from that point on she carried a can of pepper spray for protection and worried when it would happen again. Also, she was struggling to make ends meet each month. The cost of living in the city was wearing on her.

Ramla felt certain she could really do something with her life and provide a whole lot more for her daughter if she could just work somewhere that offered health benefits and good working conditions.

---Let's see...3331 Pennsylvania Avenue....it's here somewhere, She then saw the address numerals glittering in the sun on the front of a high-rise office building. "That's my ticket," Ramla said as she got off, smoothed her skirt and blouse and grabbed her purse. It was time to remember the etiquette class Aunt Mae had her attend during the summer she spent with Alice. The instructor had taught the teens how to dress for an interview and now Ramla was ready for the challenge ahead.

She took one last look in the side mirror of a parked car and saw that she was polished. When she walked inside, she looked on the board in the lobby and found that the personnel office was on the 7th floor. Ramla boarded the elevator, pushed the button and waited nervously for the door to open. When she stepped out, the receptionist directed her to the personnel office. A young woman was packing up her things for the day. She placed a rubber band over a thick stack of what must have been resumes and applications. Ramla quickly walked over to her.

"Hello, may I submit my application before you leave?"

The woman looked worn out, but gave her the time to fill out an application. "Just a moment, I'm going to lock the doors so no one else will get in," she said reaching into her desk for her keys. Ramla couldn't be sure, but got the impression the woman was irritated that she had slipped in so late in the day.

Ramla nodded and smiled, noticing the run in the woman's stocking.

"Okay, I'm sorry, but it has been nuts here today and I just don't have the energy to stay one second longer after five o'clock."

Ramla thumbed through the three-page form and began answering the questions. She was interrupted by the woman.

"Ramla is it? What are your skills? What are you looking for?"

Ramla swallowed hard and decided to be honest. "Well, I am looking for a career, something I can do that'll make a difference."

Ramla watched the personnel officer's expression turn into a smile.

"Can you type?"

"Oh, yes. I can type 65 words a minute."

Ramla was sure she had fudged on the amount of words she could really type, but she wanted and needed the job.

"Okay Miss Ramla, finish your application and I think you'll be hearing from me in the near future. We're looking for a full-time personnel clerk. Would that be of some interest to you?"

"Yes. What exactly do they do....a personnel clerk?"

"Oh, typing, filing and answering the phone, different projects. By the way, my name is Carolyn. Remember, you'll be hearing from me."

Carolyn decided to be patient because Ramla reminded her of her daughter who had perished in a terrible car accident just a few months ago. The collision haunted Carolyn because her daughter had called hours before to ask for a ride home. As usual, Carolyn was too busy with her job to spare a few extra minutes and called a cab. By helping Ramla, Carolyn believed in her heart that this was her chance to somehow make up for her neglect.

Ramla smiled, nodded and completed her application. She handed it over to Carolyn and said thank you and goodbye. She felt as though she had just had an impromptu interview. Ramla felt confident and walked like it—head high, shoulders back, stepping like a full grown woman in her black patent heels.

She stood on the corner trying to flag down a cab. To her surprise, Carolyn pulled up and asked where she lived.

"Come on get in. I'll take you home."

Since she was near the White House, she wanted to ride by in the cab to see if her mother was still there. She accepted the ride home, but returned later in her own cab to look for Eva.

She searched for her mother along the front gates, but didn't see her. An emptiness and longing came over her. She wanted to see and talk with her. Ramla sighed and turned on the "Out of Service" light. She returned home, and decided to relax.

Two days later Ramla was catnapping in the afternoon when the phone rang.

"Hello?"

"This is Carolyn from the plant. I'm the personnel officer you met the other day. How are you?"

Ramla sat up on the corner of the bed and jarred herself alert. She hoped and prayed she would tell her what she wanted to hear.

"Hi Carolyn, I'm doing well. What about you?"

From her years as a cab driver, Ramla had come to loathe small talk, but she wanted to sound professional.

"I'm fine. I would like to extend a job offer to you. Are you still interested in becoming a personnel clerk?"

"Yes, I am. If you don't mind me asking, how much does the position pay?" She couldn't think of a better way to ask other than to just do it.

"Not at all. A clerk in this position gets paid $30,000 per year. Is that sufficient?"

Ramla was floored. She jumped up trying to hold her composure. "I'll take the job. When do I start?"

"What about tomorrow? I could really use your help with the other applicants," Carolyn laughed.

"Yes!" Ramla shouted. She was hoping that Carolyn could not hear her jumping up and down.

"I'll see you then."

Ramla hung up and let out a whoop of joy. She began singing, "Money, Money, Money, Money, Moneeeey! Tomorrow, my destiny begins. No more driving cabs, well wait...slow down. Maybe I can do that part-time, just for a little while until I save up enough money to buy a house."

eight

Ramla arrived bright and early, ready to start her new career. She glanced at her watch, and saw Doris walking across the office to greet her.

"Hello, Ramla. Are you prepared to get started?"

"I sure am."

"Here, please take these forms to Mr. Cox. He's located down the hall to the left, the second office from the end. He's in the middle of hiring for his department."

Ramla took the mass of papers and memorized the directions. She felt important as she efficiently made her way down the corridor.

An employee whispered, "There goes Carolyn's new personnel clerk,"

Already she was enjoying her new prestigious role within the company. She turned the corner and counted the offices to the end, stopping at the sign that read "Cox."

Ramla walked in and was about to place the papers on the Mr. Cox's desk but it was already full and he had his head down in concentration.

"Here are the forms Doris sent," she said trying to see his face to make sure he had heard her.

"Ramla, is that really you?"

Sammael Cox. He was all man now—rugged and masculine looking. His eyes glittered from some internal heat. She felt her insides turn to jelly and her knees go weak. He was still the most handsome man she had ever seen.

"My God. Yes it's me. Sammael…I can't believe it!"

He grabbed her and squeezed her tightly. She was overcome in his embrace and leaned in close, remembering their affection.

"Do ya wanna grab some dinner and catch up after work?"

"Sure, come find me when you're ready. I'm just outside Doris's office."

"There's a French restaurant just around the corner. I think you'll love it," he winked.

Ramla floated through the rest of the day, but chastised herself for looking forward to dinner with him. ---When we first met, we were practically kids. Surely he has grown up and knows how to treat a lady. Her anxious thoughts concerned her with what might happen next; she was filled with anticipation. At five o'clock her heart beat so fast she could hardly think. She wondered if she could take things slowly, seeing where they might possibly go. She didn't want to easily jump in his bed but she knew her flesh was still weak for him. She had gained new ground, however, and a new level of respect for herself. ---I don't want to lose *everything* I have gained, she thought. She hadn't seen him since he dropped her at the Greyhound station ten years ago.

—

"So how in the heck are you, Ramla?" Sammael said as he pulled out her seat at the restaurant.

"Thank you, I'm fine. Gee Sammael, the last time I saw you, your mom was moving, and you were quitting school to work full-time in North Carolina. Fill me in on what's been going on with you."

Sammael grew silent for a moment and summoned the maître d'.

"Bring us your finest bottle of merlot."

He looked at Ramla and she saw his desire.

Just that quickly, he moved beyond it and said, "Wow, where do I begin? We moved to a small town just outside of Raleigh. Mom tended to her aunt, and I got a job as a construction worker at the local plant. I started out as a gopher and worked my way up to supervisor, then contractor. I stayed there long after her aunt passed away. Mom was brokenhearted. Her aunt raised her and she couldn't get over it…"

"Here you are sir." The waiter poured a sample into Sammael's wine glass. He then took a quick whiff to smell the aroma. At last he tasted it, sloshing it in his mouth to see if it was good enough for them. He approved and nodded to the waiter to pour Ramla a glass.

Once the waiter left, Sammael took a long swallow and poured himself another.

"Ramla, Mom died six months ago."

They both sat silent.

"I'm so sorry…she was like a mother to me too." Ramla's lower lip quivered.

He only nodded his head and swallowed more wine.

"So, why did you come to D.C.?" Ramla asked him.

"I couldn't stay in Raleigh; there were too many memories of mom. I had to find a new city for myself. I told my boss and he checked into our sister company. He allowed me to transfer. And, I am glad I did."

They made a mutual silent toast to their employer and the memory of Mrs. Cox.

Sammael asked about Kareese. Ramla proudly showed him pictures. He couldn't get over how much she had grown. Ramla confessed to Sammael that when she left them she really didn't have family in D.C. She just wanted someplace new to live as well. She told him about Ira and how he found her a place to stay, bought them food, and got her a job. Ramla was moved from the news about Sandra. She felt her heart sink. She listened as Sammael talked about work and how he really loved the metropolitan area. It was a nice, "in-between" spot, he called it -- close enough to Baltimore to enjoy the river at the inner harbor, and close enough to a major city, New York. They talked, and ate and drank until their tongues got clumsy.

"So, I guess you are married by now?" Ramla ventured casually.

"No, didn't find a woman in Raleigh that I wanted as a wife."

Sammael observed Ramla closely. She had developed into a beautiful woman. She was a pretty girl to begin with, but something in her eyes attracted him. Her innocence and naivety had departed and there was a natural, sultry look to her that made him think she was wise to the world. It was sexy.

"What about you, Ramla? Did you marry?"

"No, I haven't fallen in love yet," she blushed and felt bothered by her words.

Sammael poured her another glass of wine.

"You know, you're just as beautiful as you were the last time I saw you."

Ramla was courageous and queried him.

"Do you still hang out in triple-X movie theaters?"

Sammael was taken aback.

"Naw...that was teenager stuff. I think I've grown up since then."

Ramla was glad to hear his response. She watched him as closely as she watched her own emotions and reminded herself to go slow.

"Say, Ramla...would you care to see my apartment?"

Ramla locked eyes with Sammael and answered, "No, I really have to get home to make sure Kareese is okay. Besides, the babysitter is expensive, especially when it goes into overtime."

She very much wanted to see his apartment, and spend the night with him for that matter. But she was careful not to neglect her daughter. She had promised herself never to be like her mother who put her fleshly desires first and turned a blind eye to the emotional trauma that would result later. Besides, Ramla had promised Kareese she would be home before she fell asleep.

She had already made up in her mind to see him again; her heart wouldn't have it any other way. It just would not be at her daughter's expense.

"I'm sorry, Sammael. I have to get home. You understand, don't you?"

"Sure. Can I see you tomorrow night after work?"

"Yes. Thanks, I really had a wonderful time."

Sammael walked to her car and held her hand. Ramla felt like she was a schoolgirl again. She got butterflies being with him as she had before. She hoped it was a positive sign. Before she was able to unlock her car, Sammael clutched her tightly around the waist and whispered that he would miss her. He turned her to him and ever-so-gently caressed her lips with his. He could feel her passion rouse. He nibbled her earlobe, then pulled back and told her he couldn't wait until they met again. Ramla felt almost weak with desire, but got into the car and grinned all the way home.

Sammael was on fire and had no intention of going home. He watched her leave and drove to the seedy side of town. He paid his money, walked into the dark theater and settled in. Glancing around in the light from the screen, he saw the familiar faces. They were professional men, hookers, homeless, and drug addicts, all watching along with him. Risking that no one was in the theater that knew him from work, he reached inside his jacket for a vane disguise—his sunglasses. This would also signal others that he didn't want any attention, not even from women.

Once he felt comfortable, he began to watch the movie. A voice from nowhere whispered, "Sammael you lied to Ramla."

—

"Can't you see the demons of sexual addiction? You're causing a feeding frenzy boy! They are consuming your flesh and your soul," Satan laughed at Sammael. "Engulf him. He will infect Ramla tomorrow night with my wickedness. The only destiny I have for her is to end up like her mother!"

He turned to address Peter.

"Peter, because you had Sandra Cox interfere with Ramla's life, I overpowered her goodness. She died of bitterness and a broken heart. Isn't that sad?" Time is running out for Ramla. The world still rests on her shoulders," Satan cackled and energized his demons in the movie theater. "Till tomorrow night... till tomorrow night!"

—

Ramla rose early and stilled herself for a few moments; thinking about her evening with Sammael. She wondered if he went home after she did, but at once decided not to concern herself with it. She thought she might want things to work out between them.

Ramla gently awakened her daughter and helped her get ready for school. She wanted to get to work early to make a good impression, and to see Sammael. She combed her hair, applied makeup, and dressed in one of her prettiest outfits. She tried hard to convince herself that nothing would happen that she didn't want to happen. Ramla stood in the mirror talking to herself, "Alright Ms. Ramla, you don't know where he's been or what he's been up to, so be careful. Don't fall hard for this man. Give it time honey, and make sure he has changed."

Right after she secured her apartment, she knocked on her neighbor's door.

"Hi Judith, listen, I will have to work late tonight and my boss has offered to put me up at a hotel. Do you think you would be able to have Kareese spend the night with you?" Ramla knew it was a lot to ask, but she was desperate and yearned to spend time to with Sammael.

"Sure. No problem. I'll pick her up from the sitter's house and take it from there. You can get her in the morning. Will that work for you?"

Ramla thanked her. She was grateful for Judith's help. She hummed a tune as she made her way to work. Once there, she sat at her desk and got lost in her work: answering a flood of calls, sifting through mountains of applications, and sitting in with her boss she was in training to interviewed potential hires once she was comfortable with her position. A voice from out of nowhere said, "Ramla, you lied to the your friend about not being able to pick up Kareese. That is the first sign of trouble. You couldn't be honest about your date with Sammael. Turn away from him. Run! Go in a different direction." Ramla dismissed the voice as fear, maybe nervousness. She wanted the date to take place and threw reasoning out the window.

Doris, her boss, was a closet smoker that was easy to detect. Ramla watched her head to the elevator to go outdoors and smoke. She'd seen her around the side of the building at lunch. Doris held the smoke in, taking it deep into her lungs, making the ecstasy last. She smoked until all of it was spent, then flicked the filter onto the grimy street. Throughout the day she would come back in and pop a breath mint in her mouth. Ramla chuckled at her addiction, but knew how she felt. She had to have what she craved, much like Ramla had started to crave Sammael. She was a woman now, no longer a scared teenager. She had needs and was ready to satisfy them.

Before she knew it, she looked up at the clock and it was after five. Doris came by and sat in a heap next to her.

"Ramla, if there is one thing I have learned in this job, it is that it'll be here tomorrow. So, neaten up your desk, lock the door, and go out the back way. See you in the morning."

Ramla hoisted herself up from her desk, and walked out, grabbing her purse on the way. Once outside, she realized that she forgot about Sammael. She squinted to where she parked her car. A man was standing near it. It was him. She smiled and scurried toward him. He tapped the face of his watch as if to say she was late for their date. Ramla slightly lifted her chin up and batted her eyelashes, taking him in with her eyes. She held a seductive grin, encircled him with her arms, and gave him a tender kiss.

"Well, well, missy. I thought you were going to duck out on me," he teased.

—

Peter was getting frustrated with Ramla.

"Peter, I know what you are thinking. Remember not to interfere. Ramla has a will. She has to make the decision to do right."

"Angel of Destiny, I know that, but didn't she see her way of escape? The Holy Spirit touched Doris to keep her late, and then directed her to lead Ramla out the back door. Her car was parked near the building. Sammael was waiting, but she should have refused the date."

"Peter you are right. Many ignore the way of escape that's provided. The spirit is willing, but the flesh is weak. Faith is the key. No matter how it looks…believe!"

—

"I'm so sorry, Sammael. My boss and I were swamped, and I didn't have a chance to see you in your office and…"

Sammael held her tight and kissed her in mid-sentence. After a few seconds, he looked intently into her eyes. "Are you ready to be romanced?" Sammael knew how to punch her buttons.

Ramla smiled and hugged him. "Oh yes!"

"Good. Let's go to one of my favorite restaurants."

Sammael grabbed her gently around her waist and led her to his black BMW convertible. He held the door open for her and she slid in gracefully, admiring every tasteful detail of it. She felt like a princess, lifting her shoulders up and back and moving her hips to get comfortable. She felt flush with excitement. Sammael had done well for himself.

During the ride, the sun slowly set, revealing a harvest moon and what seemed to be millions of twinkling stars. Ramla felt rejuvenated with Sammael, they had been driving for a couple of hours. The breeze wafted through her hair as they traversed through town. She was happy, very happy, and would let it show.

They pulled up to the restaurant's valet parking. He placed his arm around her waist as they walked in. The hostess nodded at Sammael and wordlessly guided them to a private table set exquisitely and crowned with an arrangement of multi-colored tulips. The lighting was soft and so was the music. Beyond their table was a window with a panoramic view of the city; next to it a bottle of champagne rested on ice.

Ramla was transfixed by light and sound. "Who is that singing?" she asked him.

"Oh, that's a Sade. I thought you might like her music."

Sammael winked and filled their flutes. They gazed into each other's eyes and kissed between sips. They conversed for what seemed like hours. After their meal, Sammael ordered more champagne. Ramla was getting giddy and overwhelmed with desire. His light brown eyes penetrated her.

"Ramla, were you able to get a babysitter for Kareese?"

"Yes, I did," she said seductively

He motioned for the waiter.

"Check, please!"

—

Because the angels saw the evening's events unfolding, they devised a way for Ramla to escape. Since the fall, people have faced temptation and God gave them free will to flee through His open door.

"Peter, watch and you will see Ramla get out of the car at Sammael's, and get a phone call. The sitter will let her know that Kareese is crying and acting strange. She wants her mother to come home. The Holy Spirit is using her daughter to get Ramla out of the situation," said the angel of destiny.

—

"I checked her diaper and fed her. I can't imagine what is wrong, please come," Judith implored.

"Okay, I will be there as soon as possible," Ramla replied. "Sammael, something is wrong with Kareese. She may be sick."

"Oh, she'll be all right. She's just spoiled."

Ramla felt her stomach roll up in knots. She couldn't understand how Sammael care less about his daughter.

"Let's just go upstairs and relax. That way you can calm down instead of us rushing to get on the beltway."

Ramla fired at him, "What is wrong with you? Don't you care? You haven't even asked to see her. I'm not up for this. I appreciate everything, but Kareese comes first,"

"I didn't mean to upset you. I'll take you to your car."

Ramla was disappointed that their time together had to be shortened, but overall, she didn't feel good about her time with him. Not now. All he seemed to be concerned about was one thing…getting laid.

"I'll drop you off at your car, Ramla. Don't worry. Kareese will be fine, especially since mother hen is coming home."

He opened the door for Ramla, and smiled at her as they left to get her car.

—

Satan chuckled with delight, "Demons by the millions. Ramla, your God will never win!"

Satan let loose a mighty victory roar. He watched Ramla and Sammael at work the next day, determined to join them together once again. Time was ticking away, Satan would soon have to announce at what point he wanted to start the clock for Ramla's deliverance; if it was to be, that is. He commanded the demons in Sammael to torment Ramla in the worst way possible.

As Satan considered the details of the torment, he morphed into an asp. He writhed and slithered, lifting his deadly head to speak his idea to all of heaven as it waited.

"I'll stymie her with drugs, sex, and pornography!" And with a mighty force, he released his venom.

—

Ramla decided to have a serious conversation with Sammael. Inwardly and long term, she was thinking marriage. ---I know one thing. I'm sick and tired of being a single parent. I didn't make this baby alone, and I shouldn't have to raise her by myself. Today is the day, just be honest with Sammael and tell him how you feel."

Ramla entered Sammael's office and asked if they could talk after work.

Sure Ramla, what would you like to talk about? Why not discuss it now. Barbara is having a birthday party for Carolyn downstairs, and everyone is out of the office except for you and me. So, go for it!"

"Sammael, I don't want to continue to raise Kareese single-handedly. She needs her father."

"So, is this a marriage proposal?"

"Stop joking around Sammael, I'm serious."

"Ramla, okay let me stop. I have been thinking the same thing. It is my desire to do right by you and Kareese. My mother would've wanted it that way. Will you marry me?"

"Okay wait. I didn't know it was going to be that easy. What about your single life? Are you ready to settle down?"

"Yes I am, honey. I need a wife. I need someone that will lay her head on my chest at night, love me unconditionally. Will you marry me?"

"Yes Sammael, yes!"

—

Ten years had gone by fast. Sammael sat on the worn couch drinking warm beer and smoking pot, his eyes fixated on an infomercial. The job at Trucking Construction was long gone. The joint he was smoking was burned down to his fingertips so he took a last hit, inhaling deeply and holding it in for as long as he was able. The door opened and Ramla struggled as she carried two large bags of groceries. Sammael looked over at her and back to the television.

"I guess you're going to just sit there like always, right?"

Ramla was the only one working. She took care of the bills, the house, the meals, and she took care of him. She strained through the haze to look at him. He reminded her of her father.

"Thank God Kareese's at college and doesn't have to see you and your drugs," she muttered as she put away the groceries.

"Ramla, I hate it when you begin to bug the hell out of me..."

"Bug you? Bug you? Why in the world did I ever get myself involved with you again anyway? You could care less about me or your daughter. All you want is to drink, drug, and have sex. That girl had to beg for your attention, lie to get money for school trips. What kind of a father do you call yourself?"

"Ramla, shut up. For all I know, that child might not be my daughter."

"Are you crazy, Sammael? What are you talking about?"

"I mean…you've been around. I don't know how many men you've slept with. Women keep dirty little secrets. Don't worry, I hear about their stories all the time."

"Sammael, you are rotten, you're evil, and you make me sick to my stomach."

—

"Angel of destiny, why did Ramla return to Sammael?"

"Peter, her emotions were severely damaged. A soul tie was created years ago when she first had sex with him. Because she was familiar with him, she felt at ease returning to a relationship from her past. She felt marriage would mature him and ease the pressure of raising her daughter. She was wrong. As you and I already know, a person has to *want* to change. No amount of love or sacrifice can change a stony heart. Sammael thinks he knows the ways of love but his heart is cold and ruthless, and his soul is on assignment from the Prince of Darkness. He will have no mercy on Ramla. Satan's ultimate plan is to drive her to commit suicide; his assignments are designed to be fatal."

—

Sammael came up from behind. He put his arms around her waist and snuggled her neck. Her irritation quickly gave way to his charm. He turned her around and kissed her longingly while rubbing her fanny. Sometimes Ramla felt like it was just yesterday when they got married, and other times it felt like a long, tumultuous journey. At least he finally married her.

"I know what you need."

Sammael reached over and lit up a joint and inhaled it. He offered her a hit and she obliged. She breathed in deeply, just as he taught her so long ago. Her stress seemed to float away. She took a few more hits, and afterward felt relieved.

"Mmm, that stuff makes me feel good!"

Ramla gave Sammael a seductive kiss and, courting disaster, whispered in his ear what he loved to hear.

"Ya feel like a movie?"

Ramla giggled as Sammael hugged her tighter. She didn't know which he loved more, movies or her. Either way, he was miserable inside. Since they reunited, they had been going to suspense and horror movies. Sammael knew Ramla hated porn, so he had backed off of trying to convince her to go.

They walked up to the booth, bought two tickets, and walked in. Sammael brought a few joints with him, and scored some c-dust on the way in. They strolled into the dimly lit theatre, sat down and snuggled up close. Just as they got comfortable, an usher told Sammael to step out into the lobby, a police officer wanted to question him.

Ramla was terrified. "What in the world did they want with Sammael?" she wondered. Was it the drugs? Would she be implicated too? She slipped into the bathroom moving past him in the lobby as if she'd never laid eyes on him

In the restroom she entered a stall and locked the rusty latch behind her. Without thinking, she reached in her pocket, grabbed the joint and swallowed it. The police wouldn't be able to find anything on her—nothing. Ramla flushed the toilet to legitimatize her visit and washed the smell of marijuana from her hands. She was sure to escape any suspicion the cops might have about her being a part of Sammael's mess. She walked back into the theatre and took her seat.

Sammael very well might be arrested. He was carrying a few joints and some dust. Shortly after Ramla sat down, Sammael slid in next to her.

"Oh my gosh! What happened? I was scared to death."

"Ramla hush. Stay calm and don't look around."

"What did they ask you? What did they want?"

"The police said a man just robbed a store down the street, and he resembled me, a young black male wearing a black hat and heavy coat. They didn't search me because I told them I was in here with you the whole time."

"That was close."

Ramla was relieved and leaned over to kiss Sammael on his face. It was strange, but she felt protected by a man that was dysfunctional in every sense of the word. There was something erotic and dangerous about Sammael. Most of the time she was infuriated with him, but there was a thrill that caused a high, and that high was addictive. She felt a fire inside of her that only Sammael could both fuel and extinguish.

They forgot the incident momentarily and got involved with the movie. Sammael felt wild with excitement as danger and action played out in front of him. It made him think of himself. He knew that Ramla had his back; she would stick with him through thick and thin. He whispered in her ear, "You are the only woman that truly understands me."

His words made her feel loved.

Once they got home, Sammael ran a line of cocaine and snorted it. For some reason he didn't want Ramla to do cocaine. She was allowed to drink and smoke as much marijuana as she wanted, but no coke. In his warped mind,

Sammael believed he was shielding her from becoming addicted.

"Sammael, I have to run to the store."

"What store?"

"Please, I must go to the music store." At work the day before she had heard an inspiring composition coming from her manager's office. The words stuck with her... "Ain't no need to worry what the night is going to bring, it will be all over in the morning..."[3] Ramla grabbed her walkman, and ran down the block to Tower Records. She found it and immediately popped it in and sang all the way home. As she approached their apartment building, she noticed a helicopter overhead. A bright light swept the area surrounding the building. It was a police helicopter. When Ramla entered the apartment, Sammael was cowering behind the couch.

"Get down," he ordered. "I believe they are looking for me."

"Sammael, you're just being paranoid. If they want you, they know how to get you. How long have they been overhead?"

"Ever since you left. You didn't snitch on me did you? It's funny, as soon as you ran off, I heard the noise from the copter."

---

[3] *Ain't No Need To Worry* (featuring The Winans/Anita Baker) The Best of Anita Baker Record Label: Rhino Atlantic Originally released: 18 June 2002

"Sammael, I'm telling you, you need to lay-off of that stuff and we need to go to church, I am tired of living this way."

"Oh no, I don't believe in God."

"What did you say?"

"You heard me. I don't believe in God."

"That's why you're so wild. I have been listening to you instead of my inner voice. You are leading me straight to hell. I'm following the anti-Christ!"

"Ramla, go ahead with that stuff. I don't want to hear any of it. You wanted the drugs and other things just as much as I did. Don't blame me because you decided to act a little ugly. That\ is on you. You are your own woman. Isn't that what you told me a couple of years ago?"

"Sammael stop, please be quiet. You have offered me nothing but hell. My life is in shambles because of you."

"Like I said, don't blame me, and pass me another beer."

"No, get your own."

Ramla ran into the bedroom and listened to the song again and again. She thought about how her self-esteem had been hi-jacked by Sammael, and how she was small and of no use to the kingdom of God. She cried out to God for peace as she listened to the words.

The angels were interceding, waiting for her to make a heartfelt decision to follow God, and obey His commands.

—

Heaven was moved by her cry. The angels worshipped God and praised him for his mighty acts. Redemption had come for Ramla, right before their eyes. Peter asked the angel of destiny why he was quiet when he should be rejoicing.

"I'm overwhelmed."

nine

H eaven stood still. The angels were silent, listening for the word that they knew was soon to come. There were no sounds, movements, or communications made. God granted Satan permission to announce when the clock would start for Ramla to either accept him or serve the Prince of Darkness. Peter looked in the Pond of Contemplation and wondered what would happen if Ramla continued on her path of self destruction.

As he did, Satan appeared again as a snake, defiant, confident and cocky.

"Satan, from where have you come?" God's thunderous voice shouted.

"I was stalking my prey on earth. I'm hell bent on destroying your vessel. Ramla has been disobedient to your ways. I've come to declare her time-frame. The earth will be in chaos if she doesn't totally surrender her life and reach her destiny. She has one earth year to walk in your ordained purpose. If she doesn't, the universe you created will end in your book of Revelations."

"And if she does reach her destiny?" God asked, then reminded Satan. "She will become a prophet and a minister to those in the shadows that are without hope or faith."

Satan acquiesced.

"She will also become my warrior. And, any soul that willfully or unknowingly serves you will be given a last chance to yield to me through her. Agreed?"

"I concur, but it won't happen. She's too far gone. Prepare for the destruction of this universe. Insanity is her lot. Like mother, like daughter."

With his threat hanging heavy in the air, Satan disappeared and continued roaming the earth looking for other victims to torment. He had already concluded Ramla's fate and had no more time to waste on her. With all of the assaults sent against Ramla, she was as good as finished.

"Michael, synchronize the time," God commanded.

"It is done in your name, Almighty."

Michael bowed to God, obeying him and instructing the deed to be done. The Keeper of Records peered at the time set by Michael and wrote *Satan's Final Chapte*r.

—

For the first time in many nights, Ramla began to dream. Her body was relaxed, and her breathing rhythmical. She envisioned an angel in heaven. It was prominent, with one hand over the earth and its wings spread wide, glittering with the sun's light. She had an inkling that someone was watching over her. She opened her eyes and looked around, but didn't see anyone. Then, she saw another spirit. It stood over her bed.

"Ramla, I am the one they call Gabriel. You shall have visitations for the next seven days and seven nights. You must reflect upon the instructions given, and consider them carefully. I command you to fast from food during this period and only drink water. Fasting will help you spiritually pass through many doors that would otherwise be shut. It is an important weapon to use during warfare. Make it a part of your life. Cleanse your soul from the death that sin has caused. Ramla, it is important that you gain wisdom and understanding for the task that has been set before you. Don't forget...reflect upon the voice of the one sent by God." Gabriel stood over her for a few moments then continued. "Ramla, seek out the one they call Sasha. Take my words as truth and obey them. I shall return the next six nights to visit you."

Then, an image appeared of herself with others in the land of Africa. She was dressed in colorful robes, and teaching people about God and how to gain victory in their lives. It was brief, yet powerful enough to stay with her each night in her other dreams.

Ramla roused and looked from one corner of the room to another. Sammael was snoring, passed out beside her. She crawled over him and got a glass of water. As she took a sip, the command from her dream echoed in her head... "I command you to fast from food, only drink water and reflect upon your dreams." Ramla fell to her knees and cried out to God, begging him for forgiveness, "Please God, help me. I knew you once, and I turned from you. I chose to follow my own way, the way of the flesh. Have mercy on me, restore me, my soul needs you. Spiritually I am thirsty; my soul is vexed and dry. Have mercy on me. Unless you show up, there is no way out from the mess I have subjected myself to."

She couldn't shake the reality of what just happened. She took two aspirin, swallowed them and became lost in her thoughts. She rationalized that the vision was bizarre and a figment of her imagination. She went back to bed.

The alarm on the nightstand buzzed loudly. Ramla rolled over to turn it off. Sammael didn't stir. The demons that consumed him were aware of her every move and only the grace of God would be able to spare her life at this point. She got up and began her day as she did most days; to brew coffee and toast bread for herself. She reached for the percolator. "I command you to fast from food...drink nothing but water..." resonated in her mind. She put away her breakfast.

Ramla got ready for work. She hopped in her car, and decided to take the long route to work so that she could mull over the powerful dreams and figure out what was happening. All she knew at this point was that she couldn't discuss what she saw with anyone, especially Sammael. He would gladly put her away in an insane asylum.

"Good morning, Ramla. How are you?" her boss greeted her.

"I'm very well, thank you."

Ramla sat at her desk and went through her paperwork, checked emails and returned phone calls, her normal routine. Instead of drinking coffee she opted for water with lemon. She was actually beginning to feel invigorated. As the day wore on, a manager called her and asked when the next new hire orientation would occur. Ramla glanced at her calendar. It wasn't for another month.

"Hmm, I have just one new employee. Would it be possible to have her come to Human Resources for a quick orientation?" the manager asked.

"Sure, send her down here around three o'clock this afternoon. I will have her complete the paperwork and go over some questions with her."

"Thanks, Ramla. You're a lifesaver."

Ramla hung up and prepared for the afternoon meeting. She rose from her chair and refilled her glass with more water. She was puzzled by her craving for water, but not food. She disregarded her thoughts and put it out of her head.

Before she knew it, the new hire stood before her desk for her three o'clock appointment.

They chatted briefly and Ramla gave her papers to complete and showed her to a chair. She completed the forms and handed them back to Ramla. As the two talked, Ramla found herself liking this woman; her pleasantness was contagious.

"If you have any questions, please feel free to call on me."

"Thank you, I will. By the way, would you be available to go to lunch tomorrow? I'm new to this area and well... it would be nice to get to know someone."

"That would be great. I'll see you then."

Ramla shook her hand and went back to her desk to enter her application into the database. She began typing: Last name is...and, first name is Sasha, S-a-s-h-a." Ramla remembered that the young lady had given her first name at the beginning of the interview, but her accent made her name sound a little different. She froze. "Seek out the one they call Sasha," the angel had said in her vision. Her hands trembled as she tried to continue. She glanced at the clock. It was a few minutes past five o'clock. She called it a day. "Surely it's a coincidence," she said to the empty office.

Ramla was absorbed in her thoughts as she drove toward home. Her dreams continued to dance in her mind, and she took notice. She was sure she would find Sammael drunk, high, or depressed. Two out of three was the norm for him. She wondered why she loved him. It was such a long time ago when she first rested her eyes upon him. Then, he was a handsome boy, full of life. She half-heartedly smiled at the memory.

When she walked inside the apartment, sure enough, Sammael was in front of the television; drinking, smoking a joint, and watching horror.

Without looking, he called out, "What's for dinner?"

Aggravated, she plopped her purse down on the table, kicked off her heels, and ignored his question. But this time she did something she hadn't done before—she went to the couch, sat down, and tried to talk to him.

"Sammael, have you ever had dreams that stayed with you the next day? I mean...I've been having visions and I can't seem to shake them...do you know what I mean?"

She searched his face for a hint of understanding or concern, but there was none.

"Nope."

His one-word answer hung in the air like a dark cloud and caused a wider gulf between them. Ramla was disappointed. She thought that even if he hadn't had a similar experience he would at least be interested. She felt like she was talking to a brick wall.

She walked to the kitchen and began to fix him dinner. She held on to her fast. As she reached into the refrigerator and took out a bottle of water for herself, she noticed a tall bottle of vodka and a six pack of ginger ale. She glanced over at Sammael's glass and noticed it was clear liquid. "No wonder he is so out of it...he's used to drinking beer or wine, not vodka," she mused. She finished cooking, made Sammael a plate and placed the remainder into the icebox. She served him in front of the television and went into the bedroom to change into a pair of lounging pajamas.

All evening she was strangely quiet, thinking about her situation, Sasha, and her dreams. She reflected on their lifestyle of drinking, drugs, and raunchy sex. Sex, day in and day out, but no communication at all. She had a good job, friends at work, and a great looking husband that others lusted after and often bedded. She made good money. But, something was missing and she felt empty. The realization surprised her.

She actually hoped that she would get another dream and see Gabriel so that he could tell her what was happening. It was nearly ten o'clock. Sammael was still on the sofa snoring with a lit cigarette between his fingers. Ramla carefully took it and snuffed it out. She sealed his drug baggies, cleared the glasses and a few beer cans from the side table. Instead of waking him, she left him there, dead to the world. She felt led to place olive oil on his head and pray for him. She learned to do this while staying with Mrs. Cox. It was a religious practice that Ramla didn't quite understand, but it seemed to work when Kareese cried from a belly ache.

"Maybe it will help Sammael to break free from his habit," she thought. Ramla repeated what she heard Mrs. Cox say so many years ago, "By the stripes of Jesus Christ, child you are healed." Then she added her own words, "Father, please give Sammael peace, and deliver him from what ails him. In Jesus' name…amen."

She got into bed, turned off the lights and waited for sleep. She looked up at the ceiling. There was a faint light in the room from the stars. She followed the swirls of creamed colored paint and plaster. Her eyes were heavy and she yawned; sleep was near.

"Ramla...Ramla...it's Gabriel. I have come with a message for you. Tonight is the second night of divine instructions. I saw your obedience when you fasted just as you were told. Heaven is smiling upon you for your sacrifice. The only person who will answer your questions is Sasha. Have lunch with her, but don't break your fast. She will understand. Tell her what you are feeling. Ramla...find your destiny."

Again, Ramla awoke to find Sammael next to her and the sound of the television coming from the other room. She got out of bed and turned it off thinking what a nuisance and distraction it could be, then sat at the dining room table to consider what Gabriel had spoken. Why did heaven care if she ate or not? None of it made any sense to her. After an hour, she was frustrated by her lack of understanding and inability to understand her dreams and decided to go back to bed. She lay down and closed her eyes but couldn't stop the questions in her mind that multiplied by the minute. She wondered if she was going crazy. For years, the thought of losing her mind like her mother haunted her and her anxiety about not being able to mentally hold it all together was growing. The idea of insanity alarmed her and she hoped that the dreams weren't evidence of it creeping in.

Ramla felt herself being jiggled awake.

"Get up. Time for work," he grunted as he turned off the alarm.

She sat up and looked at Sammael. He already dropped off back to sleep. She was tired from thinking too much. She didn't have an appetite, so she began her day with water and a squirt of lemon. When she arrived at work, she silently blessed the mountain of paperwork that was awaiting her. Ramla imagined angels supernaturally helping her at work. Besides, prayer was becoming her source of distraction for her overactive mind. Noon came quickly.

Sasha stood over her and smiled, "Are we still on for lunch?"

"Of course we are. There is a nice little place right around the corner."

The two women walked to the deli and stood in line.

Sasha turned to Ramla, "I'm really not feeling that hungry…do you want to get something to drink and just talk?"

Ramla couldn't believe it. They agreed to both get a large glass of water with lemon and sit out on the patio. ---If Gabriel and my dreams are real, then maybe Sasha can steer me in the right direction. she thought. She allowed Sasha to start the conversation.

Sasha studied Ramla's face and smiled ever so slightly. Ramla was intrigued and asked her what she was doing.

"Ramla, I know why we are becoming friends."

"Why is that?"

Ramla was testing her. She wanted to know if she was going mad or if this was reality.

"You're having some weird dreams aren't you?" Sasha smiled. "You even had an angel visit you."

Ramla nearly dropped her glass of water and her hands began to shake.

"Go ahead, you can ask me anything you like and I will do my best to answer."

Sasha held Ramla's shaking hands and comforted her. She listened to Ramla as she told her about her dreams, life with Sammael, and her feelings of emptiness. Once she expressed everything, Ramla began to feel better. She waited for Sasha to explain the reason for her life being in such disarray and the importance of her finding her destiny.

"Ramla, I'm speaking on a spiritual level. You are here for a great purpose. God is counting on you to fulfill your responsibilities as a human being. Not everyone gets the opportunity to serve God in the way he has equipped you to serve and help others. Many are called, but only a few are chosen. You must accomplish his purpose for your life so that you can glorify him and edify his children. There is a multitude of people that are in need of your help. They are crying out for the gift that God has placed inside of you. Millions around the world are in distress, and praying for God to send relief. If you fail, many will suffer horrible deaths. There are those who reject their spiritual gifts and live a dull life without meaning. The gifts speak loud and clear and dwell in the heart, but there are few that find them. People ignore the longing of their heart, even Christians. Some are just plain apathetic. Some believe in their ability to make a difference and they talk a good game, but do nothing about it. Others die with the dream and take the greatest part of themselves to the grave. What a waste. Ramla, when an idea comes to your mind, write it down. Believe in your inner strength and the help of God to bring it to fruition. James 2:36 says, *As the body without the spirit is dead, so faith without deeds is dead.* Don't allow anyone or any circumstance to stop you from fulfilling your destiny. You told me about your struggle with sin and how hard it is to stop doing damage to yourself. Answer a question for me, will you please? Is sin worth forfeiting the plan of God for your life?" Sasha paused for a moment to make sure Ramla understood. She continued to speak in earnest and as plain as possible so that Ramla would fully comprehend her words.

"Sasha you are right. The last thing I want to do is kill my destiny. I've had many ideas that came to my mind ... it's just that trying to make something great happen is not easy, I really like my job. It seems to hard to invent a new life or a different way of living," Ramla interrupted.

"That's just another excuse to stop you from moving forward. You have to start somewhere. If you recall, I said write it down. Keep writing and share with others the desire of your heart. But do so with people who are trustworthy and can motivate you. In Habakkuk 2:2 it says to write it down. Here is my Bible, read it out loud.

Ramla read, '*"Then the Lord replied: Write down the revelation and make it plain on tablets so that a herald may run with it."*'

"Putting your vision or the desire of your heart on paper is important. You must see with your own eyes the thing that is buried in your heart. Ramla, it is important to share your vision with others so that they can help. If you don't ask, you'll never know who the Lord will use to help you. Let me caution you. Everyone will not believe in your dreams. You must be careful not to share your dreams with the wrong person. If you do, brush off their negativity. Many will gossip about you and call you crazy. Let them. It's okay. Some stay in a cycle of malicious gossip for years. They keep their focus on an individual, trying to tear that person down and lift themselves up in the eyes of their peers. Little do they know that their purpose for living is passing them by. Their destiny is being buried under their words and time is being lost from their lives while others take hold of their dreams. Ramla, love others, and try not to judge them. It is imperative that you keep your focus and your intuition. Be led by God's Holy Spirit. Fasting will give you a keen sense of the evil workings of others. You will be able to discern those that are for you and those that are against you."

Gabriel is a great messenger for Almighty God. He has witnessed people such as Daniel, Jesus and David fasting in order to gain major victories. Fasting cleanses your soul. The physical cleansing of your soul is happening as we speak. The next step is spiritual cleansing. It makes room for the spirit part of you to be strengthened. A supernatural shifting takes place in your life when you successfully discipline your flesh. You then stand on a playing field that is shielded by the angels of God. The victory is easily given to you during times of fasting. You must give yourself over to God and allow his guidance to reign supreme in your life. There are great things to be accomplished. Drinking alcohol, smoking, drugs, and having meaningless sex are not the way to victory. Besides it slows down your progress."

"Meaningless sex? What do you mean? I'm married to Sammael. He's my husband, and I freely give him my body."

"Yes, you are his wife, and under normal circumstances sex is wonderful between husband and wife, however Sammael is sick. He is using you to meet the twisted, lustful desire that burns deep within him. His heart is not in the marriage, and he is sleeping around with other women. Keep it up with him and eventually he will pass on disease, one that could easily be fatal. Yeshua is not pleased with a husband that pumps drugs into your system, is not a servant leader by supporting or protecting you, and only uses you for what he can get out of you for personal gain. He mistreats you and you accept it. You have allowed what has happened to take place in your life. Where do you as a human being draw the line? He does not understand love. Please listen to me. He really does believe that he loves you. I will not take that away from him, but the respect that is due a woman is not there. Something happened in his childhood to cause him not to respect women."

"How do you know all this? How did you know I had questions? How did you know where I worked? How did you know?" Ramla implored.

"Sometimes it takes our brains a few minutes to catch up with our basic instincts and the leading of the Holy Spirit. All I can tell you is that I was reading the paper one morning and a job announcement caught my eye. I wasn't looking for work but I knew I had to get hired. There was a reason." Tears cascaded down Sasha's face. "I came down here, applied, and the manager hired me. She even told me that she wasn't planning to hire anyone in her department but knew that I would be a great addition to the company. The night after I got the job, I had a dream. In it, Michael the arch angel told me to seek you out and help you find your way. He explained to me that my destiny was to help rescue a woman that was called by God. My spirit was called forth, and I'm on assignment to help you. He mentioned that time was of the essence. The timing of God is very important. It is crucial that you flow with the directions God gives you through those he places in your path. But, you must use discernment to determine if it is of God or if it is Satan in disguise. Let's go back to work. Tomorrow evening you're coming with me to church."

Sasha was on a mission and Ramla was curious and encouraged to see how the puzzle would solve itself.

Ramla felt a lot better since her conversation with Sasha. She reminisced about going to church with Mrs. Cox years ago. She knew without a doubt that a good church service would do her well. The day she walked up to the altar and the saints prayed for her was phenomenal. She remembered the sermon and how powerful it was. Goose bumps developed on her arm. Her memory was vivid and tears flowed as she thought about the vow she made in her heart to forever serve God. She was just a teenager then and had gradually let life overwhelm her. She also recalled the time Sammael took her to the theater to watch pornography the very next day. Her life was never the same. ---That was the devil using Sammael back then, and he's still using him today. I must pull myself together and flee from this senseless relationship, she reasoned.

Because she became a young mother, Ramla felt she missed out on childhood. She believed that drinking, drugging, and having sex with Sammael was normal, and that she was happy, well, at least most of the time. Besides, other couples that they associated with used drugs too, and since it was typical behavior for them, she rationalized that it was not a problem for her. After talking with Sasha, she admitted to herself that she really wasn't happy.

Even though Sammael was still high most of the time, he began to notice changes in Ramla. Her speech had changed; no more cursing. And, no more doing drugs. He reacted in anger when she told him that God had a purpose for her life. His behavior didn't make sense to her. And to him, reading the Bible everyday was bizarre. He was confused. The very sight of it rattled his soul and gave him pounding headaches. Ramla had decided a few months earlier to stop smoking weed. Once she began fasting and purifying her body, the very smell of it made her sick. This was one miracle Ramla never dreamed would happen to her.

Near bedtime, she hurried to her room so she could pray and seek God, believing that Michael would appear in her dreams. She drifted off into a peaceful sleep. In her dream, she was looking for Michael, shouting his name and asking him to give more clues to her destiny. Swiftly, a dark tunnel appeared in her vision. Someone was chasing her and she was running for her life.

She was startled awake by Sammael yanking her out of bed by her hair. He shoved her her up against the bedroom wall and held her there a couple inches off the floor. She screamed and tried to tear herself free from his grip. But when she did, she saw clumps of hair being ripped out of her head and stopped. Sammael put his face close to hers and told her to shut up. His breath reeked of vodka and he had a crazed look about him. She feared for her life and braced herself for what would come.

"Ramla, you so much as make one sound..." Then he punched her in the belly. He punched her again and she doubled over. He straightened her up and hit her again, cursing her for being pious. He grabbed her by her hair again and slapped her with the other hand, mocking her for fasting and reading the Bible and pretending to be better than him. He hit her again, cursing and accusing her of being too good to smoke with him anymore and for ruining his life. With each blow his revulsion grew as if he hated her very existence. She dropped to the floor and fell into a fetal position. Still he beat her, obedient to the voices in his head.

The new light in Ramla was a curse to the darkness in Sammael. He had become insecure about losing control over her life and he wanted her to stay the same, enabling him to live as he wanted without guilt or shame. He slapped her shielded head until blood spilled from his hand. The sight of it infuriated him but he was worn out. He left her in a heap on the floor, then lay down next to her, and passed out.

It took Ramla a long time to regain consciousness. She opened her eyes and tried to move her head. She felt like she had been hit with a ton of bricks. She tried to focus and saw

Sammael stretched out on the floor. Until she was sure he was completely out of it, she didn't move. His snores confirmed that he slept so she attempted to move about. She crawled away from him and struggled to stand up. The room was circling around her. Ramla secured her footing and then locked herself in the bathroom. She took a good look at her face in the mirror. She was bleeding, bruised and sore, and her left index finger hung at an odd angle. In the medicine cabinet she searched for bandages and gauze pads and placed them over the cuts and bruises on her face and neck. As she did, she heard soothing music coming in from the window above. The words spoke of new beginnings, new horizons and inner peace. It sounded like a gift from heaven, sent to heal her wounded soul. The sweet voice sounded like an angel, and gave her hope that somehow everything would be all right.

She passed Sammael and saw that boils had broken out all over his bare feet. An apparition of Michael the arch angel stood over him saying in a loud voice, "Do not touch my anointed ones; do my prophets no harm."

Sammael's snores got louder and mixed with an unusual sound that came from deep within. It seemed that he was growling. After moving around quietly and as swiftly as possible, Ramla heard a command from Michael.

"Depart from this place and run for your life."

Ramla got dressed, gathered her clothes and packed a suitcase. She grabbed her purse, took one last look at the apartment and left.

–

The angels on assignment for Ramla shook at the sight of God's precious lamb being abused. Unknown to Ramla, her death had been prevented. Her guardian angel wanted to spare her from the beating but could not interfere because Ramla had ignored the intuitive warnings and God-given signs that cautioned her years ago not to return to him. The angel was bewildered and said to the others, "Ramla, like so many other women, disregard the voice of the Holy Spirit that tells them to flee from danger. Instead, they allow their emotions to dictate their actions. The arm of their flesh is their guide and moves them outside of the arena of protection.

–

Ramla got into her car and drove away, with no destination in mind. She wondered where she could stay and decided to go back to the hotel where she had lodged when she first came to town. She parked the car, and carried her belongings with her to the lobby. A young man checked her in and summoned assistance. He asked her to sign the log book. To be safe, she inscribed an assumed name, "Faith Destiny" and offered no explanation. Ramla wearily took the elevator to her room. Memories of the past flooded her mind. She remembered how she was frightened, yet had plans, hopes and dreams. And, here she was, eighteen years later, terrified once again. But this time, she had a different responsibility. She must find her destiny come what may.

"Hello Sasha this is Ramla."

"Where are you? I have been ringing your phone off the hook. Your husband finally picked up and sounded salty, like something was wrong. When I asked for you, he slammed the telephone down. Are you okay?"

"No Sasha. I'm not okay. He has beaten me."

"Oh my Lord, where are you?

"I am at the hotel on 5th Street Northwest."

"Just hold on, I'm on my way."

Sasha raced through Clinton and onto Branch Avenue that lead into the District. Constantly looking into the rearview mirror, she hoped the police would not pull her over; there was no time to waste. While maneuvering through traffic, she prayed that God would grant her a parking space so she could get in as quickly as possible. When she pulled up, a young man was pulling out of a space right in front of the hotel. Sasha parked and grabbed her purse from the backseat. Rushing through the hotel doors, she dashed to the counter and asked for Ramla Cox.

"I'm sorry ma'am. No one is registered under that name," said the young woman..

Sasha became upset.

"Wait one minute," the clerk said. "A lady checked in about two hours ago. She was in rough shape... please promise not to tell anyone. I'm not allowed to give out any information on our guests. Promise me you'll tell no one."

"I promise. Please call her room. I believe that young lady is my friend.

"Hello ma'am. There is a lady down here asking for someone named Ramla."

"Please, send her up immediately," Ramla replied.

"Ma'am, go to the third floor and turn right. It's 301, next to the elevator."

She ran to the elevator and noticed that it was at the top floor. She looked around for a staircase and bolted two steps at a time reaching the third floor. She banged on the door, "Ramla, open up honey, it's me, Sasha."

Ramla slowly opened the door and collapsed.

"Oh my! Ramla." Sasha began praying and cried out, "How could he?" What type of animal is he?"

She helped Ramla get to her feet and walked her over to the bed. She sat down holding on to her as if she were a baby, rocking her back and forth, trying to bring some kind of comfort to her soul. Sasha's heart was overwhelmed with grief. Many times she had witnessed the onslaught of the enemy in a person's life, but this was the worst she had seen. There had to be a force of evil present during the attack. When Sasha entered the hotel room she sensed an uneasy feeling in her spirit. It was as if a cloud of gloom was still hovering over Ramla. There was definitely a stain that was to remain on the heart of Satan's victim. He wanted to stop her destiny.

"You really need to see a doctor. Let me call an ambulance."

"No! I'm embarrassed enough. I will not let some paramedic carry me out of here on a stretcher."

"Okay then, let me drive you there. Honey, your eye is damaged. It looks like the pressure from the blow you received has pushed your right eyeball backwards. You really need to see a doctor right away."

Ramla got up and walked over to the chair where she dropped her belongings when she first entered the room. She stammered as she searched through the luggage for something to put on. "Sasha, give me time to get cleaned up and dressed. I can't believe this has happened to me." She went into the bathroom and gasped at the sight of herself. The retina was torn and looked like it had been knocked away from her eyeball. The pain of it all hit her. "This is insane. I didn't deserve this... no woman does."

"Ramla, you're better than this," cried Sasha.

"Please, I don't want to talk about it right now. Let's just leave."

Ramla convinced Sasha to take the staircase and go out of the emergency backdoor so that they wouldn't be seen by the people in the lobby. They got in the car, and went to the hospital.

The nurses were furious when they saw Ramla's face. As they tended to her injured eye and broken finger, the doctor on duty discovered that her ribs were fractured.

"Honey, it is important that we notify the police," said the head nurse. "You need to file a police report against whoever did this to you. Was it your boyfriend?"

"No. It was my husband."

"Are you afraid that he will do more harm to you?"

"I thought he was going to kill me. I escaped with my life. There was red heat in his eyes, he was furious. I still don't understand what provoked him. I was asleep. Honestly, I did nothing to deserve this."

The head nurse ordered her assistant to call law enforcement.

"I'll be fine. He doesn't know where I am staying."

"I still think it's important to file a police report. It will be for the record and your protection, just in case he finds you. I've recently saw the corpse of woman roll in here. She too thought she would be okay and didn't inform the police,

189

and now her family is preparing her funeral arrangements. Honey, guard yourself. A man that beats any woman the way he has beaten you is a maniac. In my opinion, Satan himself has entered that man's soul," said the nurse.

"Yes ma'am, I will do just that."

"We will take pictures."

"Please allow me to do it in my own timing. Right now I just need peace."

Sasha walked over to Ramla and insisted she follow the nurse's instructions. The police were called, and a report was filed.

Ramla stayed with Sasha. After a few weeks, her body healed, but her mind was still tormented from the incident. What hurt her most was the fact that Sammael hadn't been violent with her before. He was a drug-head and enjoyed smoking weed, but he had never showed signs that he would attack her in such a vicious manner. She thought back to the warning signs revealed to her when she first reconnected with him. If only she had listened.

—

"Gabriel, go to the Pond of Contemplation and check on Peter. Once you have evaluated his faith, bring back to me the results. Hurry, time is of great importance."

"Peter, why are you weeping?" asked Gabriel.

"Gabriel, the demons taunted Sammael, and pressed in hard on him to beat the living daylights out of Ramla."

"I know what has happened. Sammael is doing what his father, the devil, commands him to do. God, by his spirit, has exposed Sammael to Ramla again and again. It is up to her to get free. She decided to return, against all warnings."

"I understand. Obedience is better than sacrifice. I have calmed down since I first arrived, however my heart goes out to her. She loves him with great intensity. I see how humans defy God's instructions and follow their own way, only to blame God when things don't turn out as planned."

"Peter, I'm amazed at your growth, you have gained much understanding. Glory be to God, forevermore. Know that God has made another way of escape for Ramla. Keep watching. It is the desire of our Heavenly Father that Ramla will allow the veils to fall from her eyes, and finally follow the divine plan God has established for her life. Once she learns to obey and forgives herself for all of the wrong decisions she had made in the past, Ramla will conquer every stumbling block placed before her and move forward."

Gabriel took leave of Peter and discovered Michael the arch angel putting on his armor, preparing to rescue another soul.

"Gabriel, how is Peter coming along?"

"Michael, he has finished his learning and is now prepared to be crowned."

"Glory be to God, the one that never fails!"

"There is a soul that needs my help. I must move swiftly. Satan is planning to kill one of the singer's tonight. It is important that I stop him. Her name is Mary, and she is needed for this particular season on the earth. Her music will help build Ramla's self-esteem. God has gifted Mary and allowed her to suffer many things, and she is ready for her destiny on earth. Satan has sent a legion of demons her way to try and stop the plan of God has for her life."

ten

S asha looked at her friend and marveled at all of the events that had unfolded over the past year since they first met.

"What's on your mind, Ramla? I'll give a penny for your thoughts."

"Aw, Sasha, I'm not really sure. I know that I've been saved by the Lord, but what am I doing with it? I haven't a clue as to how I should find my destiny. Do you?"

"Go take a walk alone, and listen to the leading of your heart. What are you passionate about? What tugs on your heartstrings? Is it to provide for the poor, preach the gospel, or serve in a leadership capacity? What is God trying to tell you?" Sasha reminded her about a song in a movie they saw together. They both were moved by *Maybe God is Trying to Tell You Something*[4] from the Color Purple movie soundtrack. "You know as well as I do that sometimes we need to be quiet so that the wonderful counselor can communicate with us."

Ramla smiled as she thought about the lyrics to the song. She wondered if she was worrying too much over discovering the answer for herself. She settled on doing as Sasha suggested in hopes that her heart would point her in a clear direction. A sense of urgency overcame her, and she didn't know why. Ramla made her way outdoors and walked, waiting to hear God give her instructions regarding her destiny.

She thought back to her dreams. The last one showed her taking a trip to Africa and working with the people there. She also remembered reading a news item about the children who have suffered by the hands of the rebels in Sierra Leone. She longed to help them recover. And, helping to rebuild communities destroyed by war came to mind. She concluded that it would take millions of dollars to accomplish such a tremendous task, but refused to doubt.

---

[4] *Maybe God is Trying To Tell you Something* Quincy Jones/Andrae Crouch/David Del Sesto/Bill Maxwell from the movie *The Color Purple* by Alice Walker - Movie Soundtrack 1985

She had enough faith to believe that if God placed the dream in her heart, he would provide the resources.

Months passed and memories of the relationship with her estranged husband permeated her thoughts. She had a great friend in Sasha and her hopes were high, but low self-esteem caused her to yearn for Sammael. He had tried to get back together with her when she first left, but she would have none of him at the time. Her dreams made her feel optimistic, but thinking about him made her feel like she had nothing at all.

Sasha made sure their weekends were spent helping in the church. Sunday was always a happy day for Ramla. She enjoyed singing, praising God and being in the company of like-minded folks. But, by night she was overcome with loneliness. She recently heard through an old acquaintance that Sammael was sharing an apartment with one of his high school buddies. Bob had a reputation of using heroin. She also learned that he was dealing with a woman; someone else he was beating and cheating on. Sammael hadn't changed. He was working, but still drinking and getting high.

Her mind started drifting, and she wanted attention from a man, any man. And, her taste buds suggested that a drink or two come with the man. Ramla was unaware that an old spirit was lurking around her. The door to her past was still ajar. She didn't fully resolve in her heart that her relationship with Sammael was over and there was no chance of ever returning to him.

Without thinking, Ramla walked to the XXX Movie Theater that she and Sammael used to frequent. It made her think of him. She didn't like the feelings she was having about her life and wanted relief. She knew it was wrong but she walked into the bar next door to seek relief. She sat down between two men and ordered vodka on the rocks. It reminded her of Sammael too. She began to sip and felt its effects immediately. When she finished, she paid her tab and went to the theater.

—

Satan observed Ramla and tasted victory. To heaven he shouted, "God, Ramla has failed. It is time for you to disintegrate this universe. I have won. Now bow before me!"

"Michael, how much time does Ramla have?" God asked.

"O' God, she has seventy minutes remaining."

"We must prepare for Armageddon. We do have some time left," God replied. "Satan!" He thundered, "According to our agreement, I still have timer."

"I am standing my ground here in heaven for the final minutes of earth," said Satan.

"Michael, begin Armageddon, and listen closely for my instruction."

"It is done in your name, amen," Michael replied as he lifted his other hand over earth.

—

Sasha looked up from her Bible, and listened with concern as the wind chimes outside her front door began to violently sway. She got up and went outdoors to look at the sky. It was growing darker by the second. She ran upstairs and called out to Ramla. Not hearing a response, Sasha peered into her bedroom. She looked around the room and found an old purse Ramla used to carry when she lived with Sammael. She opened it and discovered a worn address book. The pages in the section L were torn out, as if Ramla was looking for an old address. Immediately Proverbs 26:11 came to mind, *As a dog returns to its vomit, so a fool repeats his folly.*

"Oh my God! Ramla!" she screamed as she ran down the street. She passed others coming out of their homes and looking skyward. They looked fearful, expectant of some horrible turmoil spiraling downward toward the earth. She didn't know why she was so frightened and concerned for her friend, but she knew she had to find her. As she dashed, people were pointing upward, screaming and scattering in different directions. Sasha kept running. It was as if she was being led, and she had an inkling that Ramla decided to turn back to her old ways.

Ramla was literally under a strong attack. The unclean spirit that had departed from her months earlier was roaming through dry places, and decided he wanted his former temple back. He desired to possess Ramla's body again, only this time he had invited more demons worse them himself.

A scripture rang in Sasha mind. Matthew 12:44-46,

'I will return to the house I left.' When it arrives, it finds the house unoccupied, swept clean and put in order. Then it goes and takes with it seven other spirits more wicked than itself, and they go in and live there. And the final condition of that man is worse than the first. That is how it will be with this wicked generation. She knew that the spirit of God was warning her about the event that was taking place in her friend's life.

Ramla's head was spinning in confusion; she felt like she was losing her mind. Her face was drained and she felt nauseated.

Sasha knew that time was of the essence. She quickened her pace in high expectation of finding her friend. She knew the importance of Ramla's destiny, and was determined not to lose her to the evil forces that ruled her life for many years. She also knew that many souls were hanging in the balance. God created Ramla and placed her on earth to help people. If she didn't fulfill her destiny, millions of lives would be lost.

Sasha saw the old bars and seedy theaters up ahead, and stumbled when she heard the loudest and most deafening sound she had ever heard. Her ear drums nearly burst. It was a long, loud trumpet blast. Instantly, she knew it was Gabriel blowing the final sounds of Armageddon. Sasha screamed. She believed it wasn't the correct time for all of this to happen. Tears trickled down her face and she fell to her knees, exhausted. She looked on the pavement and saw blood. It was dripping from her ears.

Something in her soul ordered her to her feet. "Sasha, get up and find Ramla, now!" She looked in disbelief at Michael the arch angel standing in front of her. In an instant, he was gone. She collected herself and ran full force ahead. "Don't look at the heavens. You can't speak to Ramla, but she needs to see your presence. She is not to receive any additional help at this point. Be silent!" Michael's voice rang out. Sasha resumed running until she found Ramla standing in a long line at the theater, oblivious to what was happening all around her. In fact, all of the drunks, hookers and other vagrants were unaware. She knew she couldn't say anything to her, but just had to be seen.

A woman appeared next to Sasha. She turned to her and tried to communicate without uttering a word, "Silence, my child, I'm a guardian angel. I understand what is happening. You are not to look at the sky, but I will need to tell you what is going on. Move closer to Ramla until she sees you. Hurry child. It's the opening of the sixth seal as prophesied in Revelations!"

Sasha continued to look straight ahead, trying to get Ramla's attention.

"Hurry, Sasha!"

"Why is the ground rumbling?" Sasha screamed to the angel. "What should I do? Please help her. The world is coming to an end."

"Calm down Sasha, just trust in the Lord. The first judgment is beginning. The white horse has been set free with a rider that is a war monger. The second seal has been opened, and a red horse is running free with Satan sitting upon his back. The opening of the sixth seal has started. The black horse has a rider carrying a pair of balances in his hand and is too running free!" the angel explained.

Ramla looked up and saw Sasha staring at her. She didn't know why she appeared to be so panic stricken, but she felt convicted about the sinful life she had lived. At that moment she realized that she hadn't taken her destiny seriously. Her purpose for living had not been important within the chambers of her heart. She was aware that she had failed as a believer, began to cry and fell to her knees. Ramla was tired, and finally decided to surrender. "Oh God, I am here to receive your word and direction. Show me your will. Show me your way. Please, please forgive me Lord. Have mercy on my soul!" she silently prayed in the middle of the street, amid the chaos of Armageddon.

People were screaming and crying. The sun turned blood red.

"Sasha, you cannot speak to her. She has thirty seconds remaining," the guardian angel announced.

Ramla ran inside the theater and stood over an ailing drunkard sitting on the floor begging God to help him. She laid her hand upon his head.

—

Satan observed the scene, and became furious with Ramla. He commanded the demons inside the theater, "Hurl a thousand swords at Ramla!"

And, exactly one-thousand swords were thrown in her direction.

—

Ramla looked up and saw the theater lights flashing and called out to the name that is above every name—Jesus! She balled up both fists as if preparing to fight and yelled, "I plead the blood of Jesus. Satan, the blood is against you!"

The flashing ceased and the room suddenly was illumined.

"I see you demons. I command you in Jesus' name to leave!" Ramla shouted.

At that precise moment, there was shuffling and scurrying and many unseen escapes through exit doors that opened and closed, opened and closed. There were squeaks and hisses and whines, and when the commotion was over, all was still.

Ramla turned her attention back to the old drunkard before her, with one hand up toward heaven and the other upon the old man's head, she summoned, "Oh Lord, allow me to be an instrument of your love and help this man find everlasting life with you. I praise you, almighty God!"

Outside, the winds were still swirling and the horses of Revelations were pounding their path to the destruction of the universe.

Upon hearing her words of petition, Jesus placed his hand upon Ramla. She felt it and shrieked with joy.

Jesus spoke to her saying, "The spirit of the sovereign lord is on me, because the Lord has anointed me to preach good news to the poor. He has sent me to bind up the brokenhearted, to proclaim freedom for the captives and release from darkness for the prisoners, to proclaim the year of the Lord's favor and the day of vengeance of our God, to comfort all who mourn, and provide for those who grieve in

Zion— to bestow on them a crown of beauty instead of ashes, the oil of gladness instead of mourning, and a garment of praise instead of a spirit of despair. They will be called oaks of righteousness, a planting of the Lord for the display of his splendor."

Ramla stood there, entranced, and then heard another voice.

"Ramla, you have been called to rebuild ruined and desolate places, and to renew the people that dwell in the land. Many generations have been devastated by war. Go and help. My spirit dwells within you, the same spirit that raised Jesus from the dead. As you decree and declare what is to come, know that your words will activate the power, and the Holy Spirit will bring it to pass."

"Thank you God, thank you! I now know my destiny. It is to provide support to humanity, and restore broken places. Lord, I want to fulfill your calling and help those who have struggled, just as I did. I will find out the needs of those who you placed in my path, and with your help and direction, give as you see fit. Hallelujah! Thank you Jesus for your message, hallelujah!"

—

"Stop all action Michael!" God thundered his instruction.

Michael immediately brought to a halt the devastation of Armageddon, and assumed the pose to hold time still for a moment.

"Satan, you have lost. Ramla found her destiny and the purpose for her life. You must lay down your weapons and command your demons to withdraw their attack on her. She is free from your grip now. Your strongholds have been broken."

Satan fell into a fit of rage too powerful to express.

"Jesus, return the seals back to their former state and soothe the rumbling belly of the earth," God commanded.

And so he did and the earth calmed.

—

Jesus, by the power of the Holy Spirit, healed the man through Ramla, and appeared to her.

"My child, you have found your destiny. Stay faithful to the calling and listen closely to your heart. I will give you the words to speak to help your brothers and sisters. Go to the four corners of the earth and encourage men to seek me. Witness to the lost and give your testimony. I will provide the finances to rebuild the wasted places, feed the poor, and train my leaders. Hebrews 4:12 says, *For the word of God is living and active. Sharper than any double-edged sword, it penetrates even to dividing of soul and spirit, joints and marrow; it judges the thoughts and attitudes of the heart.*

"Build up your spirit with the word of God; hide it in your heart."

"Oh, Lord, I have one request," she pleaded.

He saw her heart and knew that it was changed.

"It is already done, in God's name, dear child."

Ramla thanked Jesus and prayed before him. Then, she walked in her new authority to see the one that she prayed for, and headed to meet the familiar spirit.

She entered the apartment and didn't speak a word. She placed her hand upon Sammael's head and began praying. Holy words came from her tongue. As a result, he got down on his knees and wept. Shame and guilt engulfed him. He felt tremendous love and a peace in Ramla beyond his comprehension. He wanted what she had.

Upon her command, the legions within him left. Ramla looked closely at his forehead and saw the mark placed upon him at birth; it was disappearing, leaving behind smooth skin. The drunkard, drug addicted sex-fiend was forgiven and cleansed. He was renewed by the sprit of the living God. She smiled at him and looked heavenward.

Ramla turned to leave. Sammael stopped her and said, "I have something for you and Kareese."

"What is it?"

205 ⮰ *Destiny's Deadly Dialogue*

"When my mother died, she left behind an insurance policy. You and Kareese are the beneficiaries. For years I was blind and hid this truth from you. Wait right here and I will get the papers for you to sign. Turn them in to the insurance company and the money that rightly belongs to both you and Kareese will be immediately sent."

"Insurance policy? Why didn't you tell me?

"I don't know why, but my heart was full of hate and resentment toward you and Kareese. I actually married you in hopes of cashing in on the policy.

"What happen? You never cashed it."

"Honestly? I tried many times, but for some reason my plans failed. The agent at the insurance company informed me that you could claim the policy once Kareese turned eighteen years old. I was going to deceive her into signing the forms and collect the money for myself. When you placed your hands on me something weird happened. Do you think you can ever find it in your heart to forgive me?"

"Sammael, I forgive you."

"I'll go and get the policy. My mom kept it a secret from me. Her lawyer informed me about the policy several years after she passed away."

Ramla stood in shock. She wondered if it was too good to be true. The words written in Proverbs 13:22, *A good man leaves an inheritance for his children's children, but a sinner's wealth is stored up for the righteous.*

She didn't believe it applied to her situation because she knew Mrs. Cox wasn't wicked.

The Holy Spirit whispered, "Ramla, your thoughts are correct. The policy fell into the hands of her son, the one who the prince of darkness turned against you at birth. He is an unrighteous man. Wealth was laid up for the righteous.".

"Here you are Ramla. The net worth of the policy is five hundred thousand dollars."

Ramla jumped for joy and praised God, amazed at the provision she was holding in her hands. She hugged Sammael and cried on his shoulders like a baby. He tried with all of his manly power to fight back the warm tears that ran down his face. He calmed Ramla and told her to go and do the work God had sent her to complete. Ramla picked up her purse and wondered for a split second if Sammael would make a good husband now that he was delivered. But the life that they once had was now over, the season had passed and the world was waiting for her to move forward.

Sammael walked over to the radio and turned it on. To Ramla's surprise, a preacher was yelling to the top of his lungs quoting Galatians 5:1, *It is for freedom that Christ has set us free. Stand firm, then, and do not let yourselves be burdened again by a yoke of slavery.* He brought his resounding voice down a few levels and clearly explained, "Move on. Once God has delivered you from a harmful situation – move on!"

Ramla knew from experience that Sammael wasn't destined to travel with her into her future. She decided in her heart to allow God to take care of him, and then whispered, "Thank you, God. Thank you." The Holy Spirit embraced her and poured out upon her a love so pure and sweet it gave her chills. Ramla put one foot in front of the other, and moved on, not looking back and wasting any more precious time thinking about her past.

Ramla paid the balance of Kareese's college tuition and made sure all of her debtors were paid in full with the money she received. With the help of Sasha, who was sharp when it came to investments, Ramla invested in properties, stocks, and became part owner of an oil company. Her wealth soared, and she became a millionaire. God was pleased with her because she didn't forget His kingdom on earth. She sowed financially into several charities and the money was used to encourage them to move in financial freedom when it came to helping the poor that attended the house of God. Finally the dots were connecting and all of her needs had been met. She was ready to be a blessing to everyone she touched. There was a burning desire in her heart to lend a helping hand to many. She couldn't wait to hear the sighs of relief and see the tears of joy from the people God had called her to. Her eyes had seen his faithfulness in her life. She knew, without a doubt, that God was for her, and not against her. She was rooted and grounded in his word, and realized that his promises never fail.

Ramla was invited to minister in Africa. Her mission was to financially bless Pastor John Mailiaka and his congregation. Giving to others was a great part of the mission that God called her to. Because of her own suffering, she developed a keen understanding of others in similar situations.

—

Peter was beyond joy as he witnessed Ramla discover her destiny. She was to become a repairer of the breach, a person who helps to restore broken places. She was entrusted with great wealth to help the poor and build God's kingdom on earth.

"Ramla's hands will extend from nation to nation. She will be known as a philanthropist," said the Lord.

Peter joined the angels as they rejoiced and praised God's name. "Praise be to God! Praise be to God!" Peter rang out.

"Peter, Jesus has requested that you appear before him in the gardens near the Pond of Contemplation. I'll go with you," said Michael the arch angel.

Together they traveled to the lush, green paradise that surrounded the Pond of Contemplation. A gentle warmth bathed Michael and Peter as they entered. Peter took a few steps and felt guided to kneel. When he closed his eyes he saw peace in the form of an intense white light. Jesus appeared before them.

"Peter, you now realize just how important it is to find your destiny. You have witnessed it through Ramla. Too many souls on earth are oblivious to the ultimate goal in their lives. Ramla and your son will teach people this truth all over the world."

Peter opened his eyes and gazed upon Jesus. "But how is my son expected to be part of this plan? He is still living upon earth, and knows nothing of the events that transpired with Ramla."

"Peter, your son is an angel of the church. He is a pastor, ministering to his congregation of believers the word of God. He was given an epiphany years ago to pursue this spiritual path, and he accepted. In essence, he has fulfilled his destiny as well as yours. You see, Peter, you were to become a pastor in your lifetime."

Peter thought back. His son hadn't mentioned being interested in preaching the gospel of Jesus Christ. Peter began to see glimpses of his own life. He remembered the private conversations between his son and his wife, and feeling left out when they discussed the Bible and the church, even though he didn't much care for either. He considered himself a believer earlier in his life, yet didn't try to challenge his soul to grow. Eventually, he lost his conviction and went his own way. Peter bowed his head in remorse.

"Peter, don't regret what used to be. Watch your son as he learns of Ramla through the leading of the Holy Spirit. A divine connection will be made between the two of them. His desire to serve is great. He will find her and bring her to Africa. Ramla already knows that she is to help finance the great commission that is assigned to him. In fact, he is already having dreams that speak of the vision. He won't question the dreams, but will embrace them as not only a sign from my Father, but from you also. John has done well. You were a good father to him and he knows it. Now, pray for him and watch the events continue to take place. Once again, fix your eyes on the Pond of Contemplation."

Peter turned his attention to his son and prayed that he continue upon his path and serve God wisely and with love. He looked into the pond and was astounded when he understood how much his son had grown. He was no longer void of wisdom but had become a true man of God. Peter was overwhelmed with love as he watched his son write down his dreams in elaborate detail and read his Bible for further clarification. He also saw a young bride who shared his son's passion for the Bible. He observed them discussing their dreams and becoming excited about their search for Ramla and the calling placed upon their lives. Each day he watched as his daughter-in-law wrote multiple pages of details and explanations that have become this book.

—

John felt peace within his heart because he had a wife that believed in him and didn't draw back when he spoke of the divine dreams he was having. Doris was a virtuous woman that made sure her husband's affairs were in order. She organized his schedule and daily reassured him of his greatness. She didn't talk to anyone about her own writings except for her husband. She knew that the pages would become important for people to have so that they would find solace in times of trouble and seek encouragement and strength during times of testing and preparation. It also helped her husband prepare to find Ramla.

One day, John was outside his house and heard a voice so powerful that he looked around to see who was shouting to him. He didn't see anyone, but quickly did as he was told. He walked into his home and was met by his wife at the door. Before he could get his explanation out, his wife smiled and led him by the hand to their bedroom. The bed was turned down and the lights were out. An oscillating fan in the corner circulated air to all parts of the room. Everything was set for his respite.

"I heard the voice too. Come on, you must go to sleep. Rest well, my husband."

She kissed him, and gently shut the door so he could sleep as he was instructed. He made sure that his pad and pen were on the bed stand.

In one long succession, all of his dreams over the past month flooded his mind. He saw events unfold in their entirety instead of in bits and pieces. At the end of the dream, Jesus revealed to Pastor John where to find Ramla and how to contact her.

He woke up and saw that it was early morning. His wife was sleeping peacefully beside him. He promptly wrote down Ramla's address and phone number. He got up quietly and closed the door behind him. Then, he went to the kitchen and drank several glasses of water. Because of the tremendous thirst he was experiencing, he felt as if he labored all night. He looked at the clock and decided that it was late enough to call Ramla. He hoped she was prepared for a miracle.

Ramla had become wealthy and was known around the world for her acts of kindness toward humanity. John heard through the media what she had done to benefit the poor. He was excited about the dream he had and relished the thought of hearing the voice of such a great woman on the phone. He picked up the telephone, then put it down. "She will think I have lost my mind," he mused. "God, strengthen me to do this. Whew…I sure hope this is really you, God." Then he laughed and said, "Stop this and do it. Just open up your mouth and the Holy Spirit will give you what to say." Finally he held the telephone tightly in his hand and cleared his throat. "Hello, hello. Ms. Ramla?" He wasn't sure how to address her, but it seemed natural to his speech, and decided it was appropriate.

"Good evening, Pastor Malaika. I've been waiting for your call. When would you like me to come to your church?"

John nearly fell off of the chair.

"You already know why I am calling? This is amazing."

"I've heard about your good deeds toward the poor and hurting. My assistant and I are looking forward to supporting your efforts Pastor Malaika."

John hands became hot and sweaty and he nearly dropped the phone. He knew that God had commanded him to contact her, yet he feared she would think he was crazy. He silently chastised himself for not having enough faith. The two talked briefly and a plan was set in place for Ramla and Sasha visit to Africa.

eleven

Ramla and Sasha exited the flight and were ushered into a cab. It was September 14th 2001 on a bright sunny day. Sasha carefully organized the trip so they wouldn't be caught in Zimbabwe during the rainy season. The cab driver was excited and honored to accommodate the American women to their destination. It was important to him to inform them about his country.

"Excuse me, did you know that years ago thousands of black rhinoceros lived in this part of Africa?"

"No sir, we didn't know that," Sasha replied.

"If you have sometime during your visit here maybe I can take you to some of the most beautiful waterfalls in Africa."

"That sounds wonderful. We would love that," Ramla decided for them.

Sasha and Ramla looked at the natives of Zimbabwe and were amazed at their ambition.

"Ramla, this is my first time visiting Africa. No one could have ever told me that I would be here on a mission trip for God," Sasha exclaimed.

"Girl, God never ceases to amaze me. Many miracles have crossed my path, and by now, I should expect anything from my Lord. Still, I can't believe all this is happening. This is truly the big one for me. My eyes have seen his glory."

"You accepted this invitation from Pastor John when you didn't even know him? Honey, you have ears to hear what the spirit of the Lord is saying," Sasha warmly complimented Ramla.

Ramla smiled at her assistant and said, "People are in great need, and we have been called to help. You shall see greater things then this and witness many being set free from sickness and disease, my friend. The spirit of God sends us to places that he knows need our help. He has supplied us with great abundance, and to whom much is given, much is required. It pleases the Father when he looks down from heaven and sees his children completing the assignments He has given. Most people think that the rich folks of this world don't worship God or give him honor, but that is not true.

God has a group of people planted on earth to do what is good. I personally know business men and women who serve God faithfully. Many of us love the wisdom of his word; it leads and guides us into all truth. Great men and women throughout history have depended on God's word to direct them. I fully understand that it stretches the mind. It also moves supernaturally on earth to bring wisdom beyond human ability to understand—widsom that leads and guides us every step of the way. The word goes out to accomplish what God would have it to.

"Ramla, you were entrusted by God to handle great wealth and to minister to and distribute money to the poor."

"Sasha, you are sensitive to the leading of God's spirit. I have thanked him every day for ordering your steps to that job...you know, the one that you thought was your destiny?" Ramla and Sasha both laughed, "Yes, that one."

"At least we both had a job and didn't have to peddle pennies in the street or dance in a bar to make a living. God's grace was sufficient for us. Even in our weakest state we were never lazy. We worked and provided for ourselves, and that's a good thing."

Ramla was overwhelmed by the grace and mercy God bestowed upon her. It touched her to know that a woman who came from such a tumultuous background could still be mightily used by God. Now, the Holy Spirit was trying to get her to speak out around the world. He wanted her will to line up with the will of God and allow him to move in her life.

"Ramla, God has plans to lift you to a much higher level. Your understanding was limited and you are beginning to recognize truths that you overlooked in the past. Your eyes have been opened to the power of God and you are seeing on a much greater scale."

"Sasha, I'm clear now about God's divine purpose for my life. It seems as if my mind was clogged, unable to hear or understand the calling and God's unconditional love for me. Others will be made free by the knowledge of what I have learned and endured."

Ramla looked different. She finally won the battle with drugs and an illicit lifestyle that had robbed her for years, and her soul was free and at peace. Each day held new excitement for her.

Another key to her success was joining a church were the pastor was a praying man, one who was full of divine power and equipped with the knowledge of God's word. The pastor stayed in prayer for hours, depending on God's strength and direction to guide his people into victory in every area of their lives. Ramla couldn't get enough of his teachings. When the doors to the church opened, she was there taking in every word that came across the pulpit. The pastor taught principles that brought balance and success to her life. She believed them and applied them and saw the difference.

A major shift had taken place. Seven years ago her life was going in a totally different direction. Glory to God that she was set upon a magnificent path that led to an array of blessings.

Ramla decided to take a vacation and relax. She had been running constantly for well over two years. Her body was calling for rest. While spending time at her home on the island of Grand Turks, she bathed in the beach water and entertained Kareese and some of her friends. For two weeks they celebrated their new life. All things had become novel to them. Kareese had grown up, and was of studying for a doctorate degree in the pediatric medical field. She wanted to become a missionary and help administer medicine to the children of Zimbabwe. She too was changed and loved the peace that settled within her home like dew in the morning.

—

Peter looked with amazement at God's word coming alive in the earth realm. The Holy Spirit carried the instructions of God and fulfilled his works. By faith Ramla's soul was saved. By faith she was delivered from a life that was headed straight into a downward spiral. This time Peter went easy on himself, knowing that his lack of understanding was enlightened and he would never doubt the power of God again. Peter was equipped for the next assignment, no matter how dark, devastating or shocking it may seem, and he was determined to believe against all odds.

Peter finally understood that God is all-powerful and all-knowing. His eyes were opened to the principle of sowing and reaping and the benefits of giving in the spirit realm; that seeds sown into the work of God were returned multiplied to the giver, and many were relieved of their burdens. Not always in the way expected, but God, in his sovereignty, saw to it that the return was beneficial on a higher level than the person could comprehend.

Peter cried tears of joy when he saw the miracles, blessings and many more provisions prepared for his son's life. He learned that obedience was essential in walking in divine purpose. Operating in one's gift and unconditional love was key to opening up the doors of success with both God and mankind. He only hoped that his son would learn of God in a more profound way. Peter wanted John to claim the abundance God had in stored for him.

"Well Peter, it is time to move on from here. You must prepare yourself to go to the next level said the Angel of Destiny."

—

The night was warm and the sky glittered like diamonds over the continent of Africa. The church was filled beyond capacity with those in search of their destiny. Africans and Americans sat in the plastic white chairs. Other nationalities were present in the quaint house of the Lord. The locals looked about and were amazed that reporters from larger cities in America had come to hear the woman that some say is "The Chosen One of God." The pastor walked up and down the aisle, assuring his congregation that she would be there to speak shortly. "I need for each one of you to give God honor for how he has met our needs through this woman.

Outside, two women dressed in brightly-decorated African clothing stepped out of a car and gazed into the sky. The wind whipped around and the stars shined brighter than the people had seen before. One woman smiled as she looked up and walked into the church.

"Wait, Sasha. We must wait until he comes for us."

Somehow, Ramla knew to stand still without quite knowing why. Inside, the pastor felt the hairs on the back of his neck raise up, and tears came to his eyes. He said nothing to the crowd that was still milling about. He opened the door and stepped outside to greet the women.

"Good evening, Ms. Ramla and Ms. Sasha. It is my honor to finally meet you after all these years." The pastor clasped their hands and gently shook them.

"Good evening Pastor Malaika. I thank you for having us here to speak at your lovely church. I can see that God's hand is upon this assembly. It is evident that you are a praying man, and many have come to hear the message of hope that God has gifted you with from the foundations of the earth...amen. Your father was a good man. He may have missed the calling of God, but who are we to judge. All of us have missed it, in some manner or another during the course of ours lives. The fact that you were obedient to his call, and the legacy that was established by God for your family didn't died with your father. You are the beloved of our Lord. I believe your steadfastness brings joy to God's heart. I am honored to be here in the midst of such a great man of God." Ramla looked deep into the pastor's eyes and bestowed on him a comforting smile.

"Thank you. I still can't believe he was chosen to observe your path in life when he passed away."

Sasha turned to her friend Ramla and finally made the connection. "You mean those dreams you were having about a man who didn't find his destiny in life... that man was Pastor Malaika's father?" she asked incredulously.

"Yes. Pastor Malaika began having dreams that he would have me speak at his church. At the time, he didn't have any idea who I was. Bit by bit, he began having dreams about those critical experiences in my life. He saw his father, Peter, witness those experiences as well. It was during the unraveling of these dreams that he found out about my spiritual path and the struggles I endured along the way," Ramla explained.

"When God deems it to be a meeting in his name, he finds a way to connect our souls," said Sasha. "Ultimately our steps are ordered by the Lord."

Ramla smiled again at Pastor Malaika.

"Yes, Ms. Sasha. When it was time, God made sure I was able to find Ms. Ramla. He spoke to me through the Holy Spirit one night and his angels told me when I could contact her. I'm living my father's destiny by means of heading the church. When he was alive, he failed to realize that he had a gift to lead people to the Almighty."

"Yes, and because you found your destiny, God instructed you to take a new surname, Malaika, meaning 'angel' in Swahili. All pastors that are called by God are angels of the church; men and women that love God with their hearts not just those with enticing words. Warriors that are going down in the trenches fighting for lost souls. Hallelujah!" Ramla exclaimed, as the small group laughed and hugged each other.

Ramla was intense when it came to lost souls seemingly bound to an eternity of destruction. She knew from experience how important it was to stand in the gap and pray for those that were held captive by the devil and his demons.

"Come now, Ms. Ramla. It is time for you to speak," Pastor Malaika announced as he held the door open for the two women to walk through.

Sasha wiped the tears from her eyes because a part of her knew the miracle working power of God, but her human nature was still amazed at the way the hand of God by his spirit delivered Ramla's soul, and brought her to a level where she could spiritually and financially assist so many people by investing in education, food, clothing and medical supplies for the needy. She had become an extension of God's hand in such a profound way.

Ramla led the way quietly and was joined by Pastor Malaika at the pulpit. Sasha took a seat to their right and faced those that had gathered. A hush fell over the church. Everyone felt the electricity in the air and knew that something special was going to happen. They stared at Ramla as she was being introduced by Pastor Malaika. Applause followed his words and then the audience quieted and waited for Ramla to begin. Since the pastor had not announced what she would speak of, the congregants weren't sure what to expect. All they knew was prosperity had recently come their way in the form of an abundant supply of clothing, food and books. The pastor was pleased with the way Ramla brought her message to his people. She first cared for their natural needs, making sure everyone's belly was satisfied. Volunteers prepared a meal for anyone who would come to the meetings. Ramla felt this was important because of the poverty she had witnessed in countries that had been devastated by lack. Now she would feed them spiritually.

John loved his congregation and his heart leapt with joy when he saw the excitement in their faces. They had waited weeks for this moment. He wanted the crowd to understand that all good things come from above, and Ramla was used by God to supply some of it. John wanted them to be "in the moment" of Ramla's message.

Ramla stood before them hearing every amplified cough, sneeze, and clearing of the throat. She stood tall and proud, smiling at them until she had their full and complete attention. This wasn't an ordinary story they were about to hear. Her life was an unusual experience that built up her endurance for the journey ahead. Thanks to scripture, the leading of the Holy Spirit and the angels on assignment to protect her life, Ramla was able and prepared to share the power of God's love to the people of Africa, both in word and in deed. She patiently perused the crowd and waited for that moment of tranquility that would allow her to flow with the Holy Spirit.

There, she had found it. Deep within the belly of the church's soul she found the silence among the crowd, the eagerness of total peace. And so she began. Ramla summoned the psalmist to sing a worship song. She wanted to hear the lyrics over and over again as if she was waiting for a profound sensing and leading of his presence. She knew that music intensifies the yearning of the people for the gospel at the beginning of service. Ramla also knew the presence of God to be sweet in its essence. She embraced the moment. A subtle wind stirred in the church and Ramla recognized it as that of the Holy Spirit.

She looked into the audience and noticed a man getting up and pushing his wheelchair aside, praising God as he rubbed his legs and stood on his feet. Then a little girl leaped up out of her seat as her mother took off the braces that helped her to walk. Ramla knew the little girl was healed and asked Pastor John to talk with her later about this family. She wanted to ensure that they would be whole and well balanced in every area of their lives.

Sasha was amazed that Ramla hadn't said a word, only her eyes had lit up, stretched wide and assured in appearance of what was about to take place. The people believed. Sasha was also caught up in the moment. The miracle working power of God just kept flowing through the crowd.

Finally Ramla's authoritative voice rang out in long syllables, "Good evening brothers and sisters. Welcome...the Holy Spirit. The presence of the living God is here and He has come to heal the broken hearted. Reach out in faith and believe God for your healing."

The audience reciprocated by offering a unified greeting to their guest. They shouted with a voice of a triumph. Many had heard about the power of God that flowed in these meetings, but to experience it first hand was exhilarating.

"I'm about to tell you about an experience that happened to me, one so powerful, so dramatic, that it will change your life forever. Forever!"

The crowd jumped as she emphasized her prediction. Sasha was smiling with her eyes closed and lip-synching praise to God as she held her hands in the air.

"Dear brothers and sisters, a miracle occurred many years ago in my life, and in Pastor Malaika's life too," she pronounced as she gestured to the young, smiling pastor.

Pastor John was excited, He was prepared to hear from God himself. He was in love with the moving of God's spirit. It warmed his heart to see that his congregation witness God's word in action. He often told his congregation that they didn't have to believe him, but believe in the miracles, they would speak loud and clear. He also said that the truth will be seen among them, and God will perform the things he has promised in every area of their lives, if only they would believe.

"Many of you are probably wondering how I also knew about the miracle that occurred in Pastor Malaika's life. God spoke to my heart and revealed the truth to me. God is alive! Did you hear me? I said God is alive!" shouted Ramla.

The congregation began shouting praise in response to Ramla's words, as sure and powerful as the ebb and flow of the ocean. The piano player was so excited that he accidentally hit a key and the sound made the audience laugh, they welcomed the sound as if it were a sign from heaven.

Ramla hunched her shoulders and jokingly stated, "There are no accidents when the spirit is moving. He just wanted to make sure we knew he was present. The main message God wants me to tell you is that each one of you has a divine destiny. God's plan for you is left incomplete once you pass away from this earth without finding the true meaning of your personal quest. It is important that you follow the divine goal that is set. God's plan is important, and it will fulfill your life. You will find true contentment in your destined, personal walk with God."

Ramla took the microphone from the podium and began making her way to the center aisle. Each face in the audience was spellbound in her presence. She wore a beautiful gown, and walked as if she was floating. Ramla dressed in gowns to remind her of God's glory and his everlasting presence in her life. They also brought an aura and great expectation to the people that came to hear a word from God.

"I need you to listen intently or you may miss a vital point that God intends for you to have. I need to tell you about a man named Peter. He neglected to find his destiny.

Look around you. Any one of you could be like Peter. He lived a long life and was a decent man. He worked hard to earn a living, was happily married, and had a handsome young son. After fifty years of marriage, his beloved wife passed away. She enjoyed a beautiful life. She raised her son and did charity work for the church. She carried out her destiny."

Ramla walked cautiously around the church, looking in as many eyes as she could. She had to drive her point home. She made her way to Pastor Malaika, and put her hand upon his shoulder.

"Peter grieved for his wife and didn't remarry. He loved his son, and continued to be a good man, but one thing was missing. It would have made the difference in his life. As I said before, he was a good man. But, he didn't discover his purpose for living. Peter traveled with the wind, whichever way it blew, that's where he went. He always had other things to do -- work, look after his son, sleep, and do the ordinary things we do from day to day. Ramla paused for a moment listening to the silence. "Do you know who Peter was? I said, do you know who Peter was?" she asked the congregation.

Certain ones in the audience looked around to see how others were responding. Many shook their heads in wonder, and softly belted out, "No." A few, including John's wife, responded, "Yes."

Still positioned by Pastor Malaika, she grabbed his hand and held it up for all to see. "Your beloved leader's father! Peter was Pastor John Malaika's father!" Ramla paused again and heard gasps of surprise and shock. "Do you know how I know this? Think about it. Pastor Malaika lives in Africa and I live in the United States. How could I possibly have known about Peter without ever speaking to him? I just met his son in person twenty minutes ago."

"Someone from the audience yelled out, "God!"

"God, yes, you are correct."

Ramla was feeling moved by the spirit and began dancing. She glanced toward Pastor Malaika's direction and saw him leap to his feet. He was consumed with the truth of God's operative power in his life. He felt the manifestation of the Holy Spirit as he danced with fervor, tears falling from his face as if he had heard this story for the first time. Ramla was full of life. She enjoyed speaking and dancing with the locals during her speech. The people of Zimbabwe loved the freedom that she displayed. Many were surprised that she was very humble, even though she possessed the riches that God so graciously entrusted in her hands. Her gift of giving motivated the hearts of many to reach out to the poor and help save the world.

"Not so long ago, I found my destiny. I was made aware of the plan in heaven once I discovered salvation, a free gift. God also had his angels tell Pastor Malaika about his plan for me. Prior to this evening, we had only spoken on the telephone. Isn't that right Pastor Malaika?" Ramla shouted.

"Yes, yes, yes. That is right," the pastor exclaimed.

"Satan made it known to God that Peter had not found his destiny. He said that people are too lazy to seek it, they procrastinate and put things off for tomorrow. The saddest part is that for some, tomorrow never comes. They die with their destiny buried deep within their heart -- greatness is buried in a grave. To further complicate things, Satan proposed to God that he create a person who would have to overcome satanic hardships and evil doings, and still find their destiny, just to prove his point. Otherwise, what good is that person to the universe?"

Ramla paused again, not wanting to give away too much too soon. One man stood up and disagreed with Ramla.

"Satan no longer lives in heaven," he said.

Ramla stayed calm and unmoved by his attempt to interrupt and cause the audience to lose focus. She was pleasant with her reply.

"Yes sir, you are right," as she tilted her head slightly forward. "However the Bible tells me that Satan walked among the sons of God, and God asked him where he had been. That's evidence to me that he speaks to God, and reminds him of our disobedience. Satan walks around like a roaring lion seeking someone to devour. He was set on killing a soul, the person he created was me. Peter learned at the gate of heaven that he should've found his destiny on earth, but didn't. His heart was vexed. In his lifetime he forfeited so many blessings and endured unnecessary sufferings, all because he chose not to seek out what God had planned for him. Can I say it in another way? Peter never followed the tugging of his heart, that desire to do something great. The desire kept tapping away at his mind, but he simply ignored it. Do you want to be in the same place as Peter?"

Ramla began to sweat. She always did this when she spoke a hard truth. She was fixed on going all the way with God's plan for the people that sat in front of her that night. Ramla realized that some of their lives were hanging in the balance, between heaven and hell, righteousness and sin which leads to death. She wanted, more than anything, for others to embark upon their divine purpose, knowing that it would introduce to their lives a blessing that overflowed into the lives of others. She understood the impact it would leave.

"Hear me church. Do you want to continue to walk around aimlessly beating at the wind?"

"No! No!" reverberated through the church.

"Then listen to me, brothers and sisters. When Peter passed over into paradise..." she paused for a moment, looking at the faces that didn't seem to understand her using the word "paradise" instead of heaven. She loved to study until she got the meat of the scriptures. She decided to remind them of Jesus's conversation with the thief on the cross.

"Remember my friends, Jesus told the thief that was hanging next to him on the cross that he would see him in paradise. How many of you recall that verse of scripture?"

Over half the congregation raised their hand and someone yelled out, "Luke 23:43!"

"Thank you sir," Ramla replied. "I just wanted to clarify that point for my astute researchers in the audience. Peter crossed over into paradise, okay; we are all on one accord, right?"

"Preach it! You are on the right track. I read that for myself during devotions this morning," yelled an older woman.

"When Peter died, he saw the rewards in his life. He raised a God-fearing son, found a beautiful woman to call his wife, and worked hard. He didn't indulge in drinking alcohol, smoking, or cursing. He tried to live the good life. He also saw things that he should have mastered. He should have followed the leading of his heart and enjoyed abundance instead of relinquishing his soul to the daily grind. Because Peter didn't walk in his destiny, upon arrival in paradise, he had to endure the agony of knowing that his negligence prevented him from doing God's will. Peter began to witness all of the souls he was called to help, he saw many perish, and discovered that in heaven, their blood rested upon his hands. He also saw millions of dollars allotted to him for the mission that he forfeited during his lifetime. Peter also saw another group of people that died because of his disobedience. Those people heard the gospel some had planted but the one that was called to water never showed up. As Paul stated in 1 Corinthians 3:5-8, *What, after all, is Apollos? And what is Paul? Only servants, through whom you came to believe - as the Lord has assigned to each his task. I planted the seed, Apollos watered it, but God made it grow. So neither he who plants nor he who waters is anything, but only God, who makes things grow. The man who plants and the man who waters have one purpose, and each will be rewarded according to his own labor.* God is the one who gives the increase. The gardener was Peter, and he didn't take the time to water the seeds that he was called to. Peter cried at the sight of their blood on his hands and stood in shame wondering what would become his lot in paradise. Sure, he was forgiven. But, he had to give an account for the deeds not carried out while on earth. His mind went back to the days he wanted to tell certain ones about Jesus, but didn't. He remembered the years he spent in great poverty, only to find that he had millions of dollars just waiting for him, not just to help the poor, but to help his family to live in peace and abundance, once he got in line with God's purpose for his life. If only he had listened. The voice in his heart cried out for him to preach the gospel. Because Peter heard so many negative things about preachers, he made up in his mind that he would never be one of them. Fear stopped him on many occasions. He was under a powerful delusion, believing that he was the god of his own life. Peter was accountable to no one while on earth. He was focused on his selfish needs, and allowed his mind to travel in circles, all his life, yes he provided for his family and stayed with them through out the duration of his marriage, but the root of all that he did was based upon his needs. Listen closely, my brothers and sisters. Learning continues in heaven. We only know in part while on earth.

Ramla nodded her head and smiled, absorbing the various facial expressions from the congregation. She learned many years ago not to draw back because of the looks. Some seemed happy while others appeared sad. Many appeared to be in deep thought. Whatever the case, Ramla stayed focused on her assignment and continued to preach. She began calling on people in the audience to answer the question.

"Sir, what is your purpose for living? Why were you born?"

The man looked bewildered and stood to his feet, swaying his shoulders back while searching the corners of his mind for an answer, "I don't know. I mean...I know God has placed me here for a purpose, and it is my hearts desire to fulfill it, but it has not come to mind."

"Sir, what is it that you love to do?"

"Well, in my spare time I mentor young boys. It has always been my desire to open up a community center and help children that are under privileged."

Ramla smiled, and the audience clapped. She looked around, and asked the folks near the pulpit if they heard that.

"This man is working out his destiny as we speak. Sir, what you are already doing is a great thing, take it to another level."

The man looked Ramla in the eyes and said, "But it seems so small. I want to do bigger things for God."

"In Luke 18:16 it says, *But Jesus called the children to him and said, "Let the little children come to me, and do not hinder them, for the kingdom of God belongs to such as these.* Teach them wisdom and salvation. Tell them how Jesus died on the cross for their sins. In my opinion, that is the greatest gift of all."

A woman raised her hand and stood up, saying, "Excuse me Ms. Ramla. I am a mother of five. Because of my duties at home it is impossible for me to save the world. So, how do I get a shot at my destiny?"

"Raising your children is a part of your destiny. Psalm 123:7 says, *Sons are a heritage from the Lord, children a reward from him.*

"Now, let's go back to Peter." Ramla led the audience through the story of Peter's experience after he passed away.

"Peter witnessed the sons of God appear before the Most High. He was shocked to see Satan among them, approaching God. Peter listened intently to the conversation between God and Satan. "Where have you come from," God asked Satan. "I come from walking to and fro in the earth," Satan replied. Peter trembled at the sight of Satan. Because of his disobedience on earth, he still had regret and shame in his spirit. He displayed doubt, and Satan felt his fear. What do you think Satan did? He tried to torment Peter, and reminded him of his weaknesses while living on earth. Peter had to learn to overcome fear. God spoke with a loud voice, "Satan, have you considered the one I call Ramla?" Satan responded, "The only way I can get to Ramla is if you remove your protective shield from around her. She is considered a lethal weapon in hell, and many angels are assigned to her. We cannot touch her unless you allow it. Remove your protection, and allow me…I will rip her apart with all the power of darkness. I will tear her mind into pieces. I specialize in torment. She will not serve you, and as a matter of fact, she will curse you and die. "Go Satan, do what you must… and Peter you are assigned to observe Ramla's life," God ordered. And so he did. He observed me while I was in search of my destiny. Listen closely and try not to miss a beat. You are about to hear of a miracle."

Ramla felt her body yield as if she was being lifted higher. The dynamics that were taking place in the spirit realm as she spoke were sometimes overwhelming for her natural body to handle. She knew without a doubt that the Holy Spirit was in the midst of them. Because of her past, she was full of humility and didn't dare to take any glory from God. She began to speak in a foreign tongue, beckoning heaven to uphold her and continue to give her the specific of God's message.

She began to tell of the miracle more effectively and more accurately than before. The Holy Spirit gave her clarity of thought so that she could speak profoundly in her native English language. She felt a rush of syllables upon her as the tempo popped and rhythms effortlessly danced their way into a communication unknown to her all over again. God had a word for the people in attendance. Immediately, Sasha stood and interpreted the tongues and events that followed. It was as if Sasha was in paradise witnessing the events.

I am your God and you are my people. My desire is to bring health and prosperity to every area of your life. Depart from your evil ways and turn towards me. Cry out with a loud voice. When you do this I will hear from heaven and heal your land. You will become a benefactor of my blessings. Freely you will flow in the power of my holy spirit. The gifts inside you will begin to operate and produce a harvest that is pleasing unto me. I love you with an everlasting love. With an unconditional love will I redeem my people.

—

Meanwhile Peter stood at the Pond of Contemplation. He watched in awe as all of the pieces of Ramla, his son and daughter-in-law's life intersected and finally came together. Finally, he was at peace with himself, and said, "Peter, I forgive you." At that moment a weight lifted off of his soul and he was full of joy because he knew that people would be given a chance to learn from Ramla, Pastor John and himself, especially since the handwritten documents that were taken with care by his daughter-in-law have become a book.

All of heaven was satisfied with Sasha's ability to interpret Ramla's vocalizations. Peter got a glimpse of what was taking place in heaven, and smiled to himself while enjoying his living arrangements in paradise, a special place on another level of heaven, in spite of his past disappointment over his own life. He realized that while on earth he was nothing but an old, stubborn man that didn't come to know God before his experience in heaven. Peter realized that just being a good person was not enough; so much more was required of him.

The angel of destiny appeared before Peter.

"Peter, you forgave yourself. Embrace who you have become since your entrance into paradise. Your worship has been accepted by the Father. He loves you with an everlasting love."

"Thank you, Angel of Destiny. You have taught me many things. Now I know that all things are working together for my good. I am a new creature now. Glory be to God forevermore."

Peter noticed that all of the fear that dwelled in his heart was finally gone, the tears that once filled his eyes were gone and his heart was elated. Now, he is as wise as his years.

The End

Acknowledgements

Taryn Simpson - Thank you for your tireless efforts. The collaborations were full of energy! I enjoyed every second of your time. I really do appreciate the dozens of answered e-mails. Your timeliness was on point.

Barbara Sharp - Your coaching and mentorship through this project was a plus. You are one sharp lady. God bless you for your professionalism.

Steven A. Magruder Sr. - Thank you for all of your support and for being the iron that sharpened me for the journey ahead.

Keyona – My beautiful daughter, the very essence of a flower

Steven Jr. – My son, when all seemed lost, you still believed. You supported me through it all and pushed me to complete the work that had been started.

Marcus - My son, my very own genius, smart guy, and helper, my baby boy, you were patient through all of my computer questions. Thanks.

Marion Coward - The woman of God that introduced me to Jesus Christ at age fifteen.

My sister warriors - Vicki Tchanque Tammy Richards, Sophia Shorts, Peggy Armstrong, Tawanda Nelson and Tracey Jefferson.

Eunice Shepperson-Thank you for listening, awakening in the wee hours of the morning to pray with me, you dried my tears with your words of strength and power. Your prayer room is awesome. It is truly "Holy Ground." Glory to God! Our prayers were answered. Amen

My nurses in the Spirit – Jacquelin M, Pam, Dionne, Yvette, Sandy, and Sunny.

To all my co-workers at *The Washington Post* - Thanks for being a family unit for me during a rough period in my life. I love all of you!

Vivian Cross (Koko) Thanks for all of your hardwork over the years, you are truly an inspiration to me.